Brona Mills

GW00496605

War
and
books

War and books

Copyright

Contents

War and books

acknowledgements

With each piece of work that is produced, there are many people behind me who need thanks and appreciation for the help along the way in not only this project, but life in general. To friends and family for being there for the most important parts of the journey.

To the readers who make writing exciting, knowing that you guys will fall in love with the characters just likeI did.

To the workshop readers who help kick my ass and make each draft better and better.

To the beta and advanced readers who help build the hype and promote the story with their own book buddies.

chapter one

Max

'I have a job for you.' Dad takes a shot on the seventeenth hole that's going to have him shoot a birdie. We both stare after the ball, down the fairways, and the LA sun shines bright in our eyes.

'Good, the company could do with some local contracts.' I turn my stick upside down and slide the handle down to the grass. I resist the urge to lean on the face and push the handle into the green. Facing Dad, I notice my eyeline matches his. I'm usually a good three inches taller. I stand straight and ignore the tinge of the muscle in my leg at the stretch.

'It's not local. It's an American woman who lives in Ireland. Needs personal security, and I thought of *you*—not your company.'

I clench my jaw and take a deep breath of fresh air and cut grass. I've not been on an overseas job yet since discharge. Most of the company's past work was a few nights scattered around the country. And more paperwork and setup than I could have ever imagined. 'We should have got here first thing this morning. My game's always better before the day's problems have had time to surface.' I adjust my sunglasses and walk towards the golf cart and slide into the driver's side.

'You interested?' Dad stows his stick in the bag before jumping into the seat next to me.

The golf cart darts forward as my leg adjusts to the pressure I've put on the pedal. Healed bullet wounds still cause muscle spasms that catch me off guard—especially when I've been slouching all day.

Dad chuckles. 'It's a driving job but maybe I can tell them you only run security.'

5

I turn to him as we take a bounce over the road, heading to the hole. 'Which one is it?'

'Personal security primarily. Bernard Rock is looking for someone to mind his daughter.'

'Argh,' I drone as the wind hits my face and gives me a moment to catch up with my thoughts. 'I'll see if I can spare someone from operations. Maybe the Rock name will help. People like to meet sports personalities and get paid for it. We're still recruiting staff for the bigger jobs. I'm sure this one won't be hard to fill.'

'It might be good for you to manage personally. You're used to being on tour, and being at home is making you feel useless. I can tell.'

'I'm not the best person to babysit some rich kid. I don't have the bedside manner to protect someone who doesn't realise I'm risking my life to do so.'

Dad shakes his head as we park the cart and he steps out. Slouching under the roof of the cart, he bends in to talk to me as I stay seated behind the wheel. 'Don't tell your mother you're risking your life. You're still her little boy, and she's no problem wrapping you in cotton wool and letting you live in the basement.' Dad pinches my cheek, but I swat his hand away as he retreats.

'Not funny.'

'Certainly wasn't funny when you arrived home from the army on an ambulance flight. That woman never took a damned breath the entire way to the airport.'

I pull my eight-iron out of the bag, stomach rumbling. I would rather call this game and head to the clubhouse for a BLT sandwich and coffee. Once I think too much, I can never win a round. 'She's lived through some pretty hairy shit in her life. Your own little life and death encounters over the years, included.'

Dad wraps an arm over my shoulders and pulls me in for a noogie, ruffling my head. He dodges out of the way when I nearly take him to the ground. 'You're not going to be content sitting at home with us.' He chuckles. Neither of us has taken a step towards the balls that have landed and rolled on the green, waiting for us to sink into the hole. This is our usual game style. Attempt to play while we talk and end up abandoning the game midway.

'Orchid Rock is in town for two more days before she flies back to Ireland. Go meet the family and talk about the job. Her father was relieved when I suggested you. He'd love for an American soldier to fill the role.'

I pop my unused stick back into the bag's holder and lean against the cart. I try to find some chip of paint or dent in the new machinery that I can concentrate on, rather than let work consume me, but the carts are polished and in pristine condition.

I don't think I've finished a round of golf in the last year. Every time we come out here, my head gets distracted. Months of talking through the new company were an exciting distraction. But the quiet days of overthinking the decisions in my life that led me to become a soldier and kill and almost be killed have me wrap up the game sooner and pretend everything is fine.

'Honestly—rich kid, entitlement, weird name. I already know I'll get myself fired by the end of the first week. And unless it's a business class flight with a return ticket, it won't be worth the bother.'

'Says the twenty-five-year-old golfing in the middle of a working day. Now who's being spoiled? Don't worry, you can always go to work with your mom in the morning. Make some coffee, help her tidy the office.'

'Does Abigail still work there?'

Dad nods.

'Then I better stay far, far away. She hates me.'

Dad checks his watch. 'I'm going to be late for work if we don't wrap this up. Got this night shift thing going for the next couple of months.'

He has hours before he needs to leave for work, but I appreciate him ending the game for me. I hate to always be the one ruining the day.

Astrid and Bernard Rock are everything you could imagine from sixty-year-old reality TV stars.

Their previous careers are over, and they are scrambling to stay in the public eye to get as much exposure and cash as their lives are worth.

The family has always been nice, but their perpetuity to overspend their million-dollar salaries means they have been chasing work for years to keep up with their own standard of living. Multiple homes in the US and a couple overseas that the kids my age have purchased as vacation homes, along with expensive cars and plastic surgery, clothes and jewellery, means that they have to keep earning to keep their heads above water. And in today's society of reality TV and social media, it means selling part of their soul to get what they need and want.

It's working. High TV ratings mean more sponsorship and commercial money for the network, which means good contract negotiations. Which means a deeper shade of tanning and a thicker layer of makeup because every day for them is a day on TV. Along with more ridiculous fashion statements, pieces of clothing that look out of place on the street but good for the TV screen.

They've had to pull the whole family in on the act. For the past ten years, with reality TV in their homes, their four children have careers that require them to sell their privacy in exchange for airtime and endorsement deals.

And they have a fifth child whom I never knew existed.

Orchid Rock has never been on their TV show. I'd remember seeing her if she was. Hell, I might have even stalked her all the way to Wembridge Studios had I known she existed.

She's not only hot and attractive and has a gorgeous face, but she's beautiful. Body language and first impressions were some of the things that kept me alive the past few years. Being able to walk into a room and read the emotions in the air.

Orchid is a beauty inside and out. I can feel it from here.

Through the archway from the kitchen, looking out towards the dining area, there's an argument brewing between her and her parents. Everyone is talking while waving their hands about trying to enhance their point, and Orchid is shouting, banging on the table to be the most effective arguer, but she still looks beautiful—vulnerable. She's losing whatever argument they're having, and she knows it.

She's just not going down quietly.

I love that.

One of the show's producers is sitting at the table. I forgot his name. Damn, I should have researched this job better.

The house is packed with people. Not ideal for a family with security issues. Often these things can be linked to an inside leak. One security guard from the gated community was posted at the main gate to the Rock family home, and I was escorted into the house by a stressed-out assistant, who handed me over to a younger, less stressed escort when I got inside the home. I saw at least two assistants in the downstairs office, not to mention the camera crew who seem to be taking a break from the real family drama that's unfolding in the house. Two camera operators, a sound girl, and a producer are drinking coffee on the outside decking area, closed out to the argument unfolding inside.

All the Rocks' adult children are standing at various places around the kitchen, in full TV makeup and hairstyle. Elvis, the eldest brother, is leaning against the breakfast bar, a part of the main conversation with Orchid and her parents, but far enough back that he's not imposing. Younger brother Ali, named after Mohammad Ali, is eating something straight from the pot at the stove, while his new wife is bouncing their baby on her hips, walking back and forth. I should know her name, but I forgot. I don't watch the show, but their names are talked about around these parts all the time. Sometimes good, but mostly jealous bad-mouthing. The two other Rock daughters, Adhara, the main star that *Reality Rock's* was originally based on, as well as Coco and their boyfriends or husbands or whatever are dotted around at various places. Trying to be part of the family conversation, but they give Orchid and her parents and the producer space to speak. I count five other kids floating between Elvis at the stove, trying to grab a taste of what's cooking and disappearing into the pantry for more supplies.

I knock on the wall to alert them to my presence and wait. I make eye contact with Orchid and open my mouth to introduce myself.

9

'No.' She shakes her head at me. Some loose blond hair has escaped her hair tie and is falling at the side of her face, framing it like a picture. She shoves her chair out of the way and scrambles to grab her phone off the table.

'There she goes, running off to the little pool house like usual,' Ali's wife shouts.

Orchid turns and her face drops. 'That's rich coming from you, Sabrina. You used to run into that pool house with me all the time in high school to avoid the drama. But now what? You got some little fan base and your own app after fucking my brother that you've just what? Signed up to the dark side?'

'That's enough, Orchid,' Bernard shouts from the table.

Orchid throws her hands out towards her sister-in-law. 'I'm not staying here for the fake friends and drama.' She points to the TV crew on the patio. 'And I've never been okay with being paraded on TV, either. It's easier if I just go home.'

She's not power dressed for this confrontation like her mother is. Orchid has a one size too big zipped hoody hanging loose over a tight tank top and fitted jeans. She looks like she pulled the clothes together in a rush, but those jeans highlight her shapely legs and I wonder if she put more effort into her appearance than she is letting on.

The file says she's three years older than me. Twenty-eight. But she could pass for younger. She's angry and upset and looks like she is trying to hold her resolve in a situation she knows she doesn't have control over.

Her cheeks are flushed, and her voice in that one word sounded like it might crack, but the air of confidence around her—being able to navigate a world where even when you're an adult your parents' careers still impact you—is inspiring.

And coming from me, that's a compliment.

Ali's wife hands the baby over to him and walks towards Orchid.

'Leave her, Sabrina,' Ali calls after his wife. 'She doesn't want to stay here, so why keep asking her?'

Sabrina ignores her husband and takes Orchid's hand. 'I'm not a fake friend, Orchid. I used to be your best friend. And I can help you with the TV thing if you're nervous about being back here all the time. We can have our own episodes about bringing you back to the city and introducing you to the public. It will be epic.' She smiles, but Orchid is not into any of it.

My mother used to tell me about love at first sight. How you don't have to know someone to fall in love with them. I thought she was talking shit. You know, divorced and all.

Now I understand what she was talking about.

I've walked into a room, and I've fallen in love.

There's a feeling deep down that I'm going to marry this woman.

But she's running out the door.

'I'm Max,' I tell Orchid as she breezes past me, the air moving between us, and I try to hide my sharp inhale as I smell the subtle floral perfume that floats around her.

'Sorry you got dragged down here.' Her SoCal accent is softer than expected—it must be her time overseas.

Sabrina calls out after Orchid. 'It's not safe for you in Ireland. How much more proof do you need that you have to come back to us?'

Orchid's out of the house and sliding the patio door closed behind her. And I'm staring out at the glass walls, watching her strut with her head held high all the way to the back of the Beverly Hills garden.

Standing in the stale kitchen that a designer was probably paid a small fortune to come up with the bright idea of chocolate brown cabinets to match the cream granite countertops and dining furniture, I wonder if I should just take a career in decorating instead. It would be simpler. Even my grandmother has declared herself an interior specialist. Hell, it could have been her that made up this room.

Orchid's mother, Astrid, stays in her seat and leans over to talk to the producer while Orchid's father, the retired sports personality, approaches me. The other family members who were around the kitchen scatter out of earshot and take seats at the table

11

with their mother. An assistant comes in from the hallway and knocks on the back doors to alert the filming crew to set up in the house.

I've already met Bernard Rock, so he doesn't waste time with formalities. Hell, I only wore a suit today because I was going to accept this job for the company, but pass it over to one of the other guys.

In front of me, pacing from foot to foot, the two-hundred-pound linebacker is scared. Worry lines crinkle around his eyes, and he looks older and paler than the last time I met him.

'I'm not sure where to go from here,' he stumbles to get the words out. 'Guess it's to be expected when your kids grow into adults. You can't always force them to do what you need them to.'

I nod. 'I'll take the job.'

'You will?' His stance relaxes as if I've just saved his daughter from any harm that's going to come her way. 'But I—'

'You were the one paying, right? And she needs protection. I've read the case file.' Actually, I skimmed it and passed it on to James to reassign. 'I'll send you a tender offer to be reassessed at the end of six months. We take it on a month by month at that stage. I'll be at the airport when Orchid's due to leave.'

Astrid and the producer stop talking and Mrs Rock stands and joins her husband.

Mrs Rock smiles and shakes my hand. 'We already changed her flight details yesterday. The studio is lending us the jet instead. Thank you for not quitting on us before we even get started. We've waited for months before hiring security against her wishes.' Mrs Rock waves her hand to the table behind her. 'But we sent your company over a copy of the threats we've received. And some minor incidents that are of concern. I'm sure Orchid will forgive us eventually if she just took it seriously. She's part of the family, whether she likes it or not. You're going to have some resistance with her.'

'I'm a soldier.' I smirk. 'Rich kids who think they are invincible are a vacation for me. I've got things to organise, so you'll excuse me.'

I follow Orchid's example and walk out of the room with my head held high, but I know I'm in deep shit.

In the driveway, I text my dad.

Took the job. Flight out tomorrow.

Just as well your mother sorted out a work visa for you. You forget we know you better than you know yourself.

Thanks. Tell mom I'll need to spend the night packing, but we can order takeout and eat with you at work tonight—if you're actually going to take a dinner break?

Already cooking up a farewell storm, and I called in sick *cough* don't tell anyone *cough cough*

Beer?

Cooling

Strippers?

… not funny

Sorry

Dublin is an hour's flight over to London. Make sure you visit my parents or they'll come to you. Remember, that's a threat no lad wants from his grandparents.

Will do. Thanks for taking the night off.

My phone pings and I get an email with the flight details from Mrs Rock. Wembridge studio isn't lending the company jet. Orchid is flying back to Ireland in the Wembridge family jet. Impressive.

Dad texts again. **You're welcome.**

chapter two

Max

At 6:30 a.m., I've completed a sweep of the jet, exchanged pleasantries and catch-up conversations with the pilot and crew, and have my bags stowed, waiting for Orchid and her entourage.

The car pulls up at 6:45, and I run down the stairs to meet her on the tarmac. I wasn't expecting her to be on time or alone.

Orchid gets out of the car, dressed in sweatpants and an overly large leopard print sweater, and shakes her head at the sight of the jet on the runway.

'Not big enough for you, Orchid?' I quip, hoping to get a smile out of her.

She turns to me, hand on her hip. 'It's ridiculous for just me.'

I smile tightly. 'Ah, but there are two of us. Therefore, totally acceptable.'

She mock laughs. 'Oh, you're not coming. I'm going home, to my house, all by myself and I'm going to forget I've anything to do with this ridiculous circus that's a family.'

The wind blows strong, and she tucks her hair out of her face, behind her ear, but I see her hand shaking.

Maybe making jokes to get to know each other isn't the best tactic right now.

The driver pulls an overnight bag out of the trunk and passes it to me at the side of the car and returns to the trunk for the rest of the bags.

'Your family has had some serious security issues of late. They want to keep you safe, especially if you're living alone.' I turn to the driver, who is closing the trunk. 'Where's the rest of your luggage?'

Orchid points to the bag in my hand. 'That's it.'

'I must admit I was expecting a whole host of clingers to be travelling with you. You know, friends and boyfriends, and hairdressers and makeup artists, and fifty bags between you.'

'You've worked for my sisters before, I see?'

I roll my eyes. 'No, this is my first celebrity job.'

'I'm not a celebrity, and you're not hired.'

'The manifest has the two of us on it. If you want to get home tonight, it's going to be on this plane with me.' I walk up the stairs of the plane with her bag, not waiting for her to go first. Maybe she's more spoiled than I thought.

'You're not staying in my house,' Orchid yells as she enters the plane.

I stow her bag and take a seat in a cream leather recliner that can go back as far as the mini conference table in front of me will allow.

I nod and pull out my phone. 'Your family assistant already planned for a car and other items I detailed to be delivered to your property.' I open the email that details Orchid's home layout and second residence on the land and my new, all-inclusive accommodation for however long this gig lasts. 'There's a cottage on your property site. I can stay there if you prefer. The layout and proximity to the front door will work. I don't even need to be in your house. Oh.' I pause. 'And I put dibs on the plane.'

'Dibs?' She puts her hand on her hip, her long blond hair bobbing in the ponytail at her back.

'If you fire me, I get to ride the private jet back home.' I wink at her. 'Your dad already paid me upfront for six months. It was my condition for taking on a rich kid case. So don't think you're going to piss me off by firing my ass any sooner. Bank transfer cleared last night.'

Her eyes bulge and she types on her phone. When she gets a reply to her message, she moves to the back of the plane and I hear her curse as she throws her phone in her seat and then storms back to me.

15

War and books

'Since it's your first time on a private jet, I'm going to indulge you and let you come for a trip over the pond.' She taps the mahogany table in front of me. 'Enjoy the fruits of your non-labour. Have some free drinks and ridiculously good airplane food. But you're more than welcome to stay put and hitch the ride straight back here.'

Orchid straps into a chair near the middle of the plane. She spreads her arms out on each side of the thick armrests and closes her eyes.

I'm not going to bother telling her that those seats go all the way back. A full horizontal bed can be made from them.

Hell, I'm a little pissed that she's just assumed I haven't ridden in a private jet before. She what? Looks at a person's job title and makes assumptions about them? I wore my best suit today to make a good impression. This shirt is a designer. It cost more than a soldier's week's wage. At least now, with the security company three years into business, I'm earning more than I did risking my life for the whole damn country.

Monique, the only galley crew out here, closes the doors to get ready for take-off.

I could piss Orchid off by taking the seat next to her, but when I look at her with her eyes closed, I can see that she genuinely needs a minute to herself.

I should go easy on her. She's been forced to take a stranger home with her. Someone to live on her property and invade her life. Looking around and snooping into her life, all to keep her safe from people snooping around and invading her space.

Once in the air, and the seat belt light goes off, Orchid pushes her seat back to an almost horizontal position and curls into a ball, her hands tucked under her head. She keeps her eyes closed and looks like she's settling in for the entire eight-hour flight.

At the back of her seat was a wall and two doors separating the second half of the jet from this formal seating area.

Monique is opening refreshments in the galley, but I shake my head at her when she preps a tray of snacks.

'Just give me a second,' I tell her.

I clear my throat as I'm approaching Orchid's chair, holding on to the leather high backs of the other seats as I make my way the few feet across the space to her.

'Orchid,' I say.

'Don't call me that.' Her voice is tight.

'Sorry, Ms Rock,' I say to the woman who is only three years my senior. 'I just wanted to let you know there is a bedroom behind you. If you want to get more comfortable.'

Ms Rock shakes her head and rubs a tear from her eye as she sits up and looks at me.

'Don't call me Orchid. I work under a pseudo-name. Molly.' She tries to smile at me, but it's cut short when she has to swallow the tears back. 'It's kind of worked its way into my life at home, so when we're out in public, you need to call me Molly. No one there knows my real name.'

I stand straighter. 'Huh.'

Her tears are replaced with indignity. 'You don't approve?'

'No, was just thrown because you think of your house in another country as home.'

She clenches her jaw. 'I have my own life there, where none of their reality TV bullshit touches. Until now.' She waves her hand over the space between me and her. 'What are you, some kind of model/actor-turned security guard?'

I shake my head and the pissed-off side of me no longer wants to go easy on her. 'US Army, discharged. Private security CEO and start up venture specialising in overseas trips for US citizens.'

'Huh,' she says. 'You look like you could be an actor playing the part of security guy.'

'I'll take that as the insult I'm sure you meant it as.'

She shakes her head. 'Sorry, no, that's not what I mean. I just meant—actually nothing, never mind.'

'What did you mean?' My no-nonsense army tone is harsh and I cross my arms. 'You think because I'm younger than you, I can't do my job? That I can't run my business? My company might be new to the private industry, but I can assure you, I've fought worse things

17

than I'll ever need to with protecting rich clients from murder plots or kidnappings.'

Her face falls. 'What?'

Shit. Didn't anyone explain to her what's going on with her family right now?

'Sorry, Ms Rock, that was unprofessional of me.' I sit on the arm of the seat across from her. 'I didn't mean to imply any of those things were pertinent to this aspect of the case.'

She nods. 'My dad says there were some break-ins at their house.'

'Yes,' I tell her. 'And some threatening letters to the studio targeting your family. Some outlined individual members of the family, including you.' No point in keeping the truth from an adult. 'It looks standard enough, and I actually have a department that deals with threats and criminal profiling.' I raise my eyebrows at her, waiting for her to be impressed. 'It doesn't appear to be anything to panic over. But your parents want the same level of security on you as they do for themselves and your siblings. Since you only have a monitored alarm system at your home, it would be negligent not to have someone with you, at least until this potential threat is neutralised.'

'Okay then.' She sighs and lies back in the seat.

'Bedroom.' I nod behind her before I turn and go back to my seat.

'I meant you're hot,' she calls out.

I'm stopped in my tracks, and despite knowing what I heard is wrong, my heart can't stop racing in my chest. 'Excuse me?' I turn to face her.

'I didn't mean you looked like you couldn't do your job. I mean, you're very attractive. And I don't want that to be taken the wrong way.' She shakes her head. 'I obviously shouldn't have said anything, but I was thinking how you had a face for TV or how you would be a young hot muscular security guy in a romance novel cover, and I was speaking before I realised how inappropriate it would sound. But then you thought I was being offensive. Actually, I guess I was. If you're going to work for me, I was being totally offensive to an employee. But I don't want you to think I was doubting your work capabilities.'

My face has blushed. I know it has. Orchid Rock thinks I'm fuckable material or something with fancy book-worthy words.

I have to divert my eyes from her. Opening an overhead bin, I pull out a Nordstrom blanket emblazoned with the KLW family logo and hand it to her. 'If you're not taking the bedroom, might as well get comfy out here.'

'Don't you think it's ridiculous, though, the life my parents have that they think they can just click their fingers and have the studio pay for security and fly their daughter around on the studio jet?'

'Your father's paying me, not the studio. Security isn't a billable expense outside their filming schedule.'

'Really?' she asks. 'How much did you cost?'

'A lot. And a favour, too. The entertainment industry is not what I set out to work with. And by the way, this isn't the Wembridge *studio* jet. That's reserved for corporate trips. This'—I wave my finger around the walls of the smaller, but plusher jet—'is the private Wembridge, Lewis, and Knight families' jet. Your dad had to pay the crew, airport fees, fuel, and pull in a favour to use it. So how about taking the security issue as seriously as he is. It will make our working life so much easier when we get you home.'

I don't wait for her to answer. I head straight for Monique, who is sitting in the galley area, draw the curtains to separate us from the main cabin, and fix myself a drink.

Once I down the whisky, I pour myself a Coke and ice, and Monique catches me up on her daughter's schooling. She asks me all sorts of questions about life after the army and the new business. I stay in the galley to avoid any more conversations with Orchid and pray she goes to sleep. After about an hour of small talk and raiding the snacks cabinet, Monique shoos me out of the way so she can prepare the in-flight meal and I grab another Coke before I go back to my seat.

Orchid is curled on her side with the blanket tucked around her, but her fists are clenched tight. I watch her for a second and realise she's asleep.

19

I go over to her and try to slowly open her hands. To let them stretch out of the vice-like grip she has on the blanket. Girl's going to get serious pains when she wakes.

Her hands loosen up, but she doesn't stir.

On the couch, I lay open the Rock security file and slip through to the copies of the death threats and angry letters that were sent over the last month. Mail has arrived at both the Wembridge studio and the Rock family home.

Orchid is mentioned by name in a lot of the threats. Which is a significant concern given that she doesn't work on the show. But the content of the person threatening the family comes from the fake aspect that they feel the Rocks are portraying in their show and in their life.

It's probably true. It's how 'reality' shows work. But it's still nothing to be killed or tormented over. Which is exactly what this person is trying to do to the Rock family.

It's uncommon these days, as the passive-aggressive things are usually on social media now. Written by the aggrieved and sent directly to the inbox or public shaming wall of the person they are targeting.

This is a high level of autonomy that the person is putting into threatening the Rocks, which means if they follow through with any of their threats, they are already trying to hide the evidence of their frustrations.

One report shows that there was an individual who was found snooping around Astrid Rock's bedroom, attempting to steal some of her underwear. When caught and questioned, he said he was paid to steal it and only assumed that the guy had a hard-on for Mrs Rock.

After the break-in, the security firm was officially set up on the property and have placed a high alert for the whole family.

I handed over a file copy to my team to start a threat profile and liaise with the other security firm. Fresh eyes are always a good thing. Since they will concentrate on the family in LA and my team is dealing with the overseas client, there should be no foreseeable conflicts.

All I can do from an investigative angle right now is wait.

I dim the lighting on the plane, pull open the Kindle app on my phone, and download all of Orchid's books. Her pseudo name was in the file, but I never thought of reading her work. She has thirteen romance books on the virtual shelf. I buy them all and open up the first one.

chapter three

Orchid

I wake up on the plane. My body aches. I'm used to waking up tense and rigid, but never in this awkward position. I should have taken the bed like Max suggested, but I didn't want to sleep the entire flight. I have to make up the lost work time from the last few days in LA. Some birthday celebration that turned out to be.

I twist my watch around and it's already 11:00 a.m.

Fuck, fuck, fuck.

I've slept longer than I should've.

The panic of the time lost has me jumping off the seat, but I get caught in the seat belt. A sharp pain across the top of my legs chafes my skin and I moan, trying to keep down the urge to scream like a girl, and drop back into my seat.

I'm officially awake now. I slide the belt buckle back and the adjoining end slips out onto my lap, while I wait for the rest of the sting to subside.

Max is sitting two rows in front of me, near the cockpit. His head is tilted, looking around the side of the other chairs. 'All okay over there?'

Why is he being nice to me? I'm such a bitch when I'm exposed to the LA vibe for too long, and it takes a while to get out of that headspace.

I'll need lots of coffee and a *zip it, lock it, put it in your pocket* policy from now on.

'I didn't mean to sleep for so long. I have to work,' I tell Max.

I shouldn't have even attempted to sleep. I'll lose the whole working day tomorrow with jet lag, but I can't write when I'm pissed off.

Slowly this time, I stand and stretch, the middle of my sweater riding up my stomach. I turn my back on Max so he doesn't get a glimpse of my naked flesh and I let a yawn take over. Bad enough I've already told my new employee how hot I think he is. No need to add fuel to the sexual harassment evidence he could gather.

I give myself a minute to enjoy the stretch and let the tiredness leave my foggy head before I pull my travel bag that Max stowed for me out of the overhead bins and retrieve my laptop. I need to find an outlet.

The front of the plane where Max sits has tables and less *sink-in-and-fall-sleep-chairs*, so I make my way over to him and sit down. I let my fingers move over imaginary keys in mid-air, while I boot my computer, sort of like a warm-up I do to stretch my fingers before a marathon of hopefully four hours and thousands of words. Max sits silently across from me, his attention fully on his phone. He's reading something, a document maybe. Every minute or so, his finger pushes the volume key on the side, skipping a page over.

'Your company is only a couple of years old? How many people do you have working for you?' I ask him.

'None.' He looks over the top of his phone. 'There are two of us who head up operations as partners. Everyone else we hire on a case-by-case commission—all servicemen I've worked with before. Means we don't have the output of wages in the beginning, and the freelancers are motivated by a payment bonus structure. There're a couple of good workers we would love to bring in as partners on the next round of expansion, so right now everyone is working for the good of building a brand.'

I nod, not really knowing where else to take this conversation. I bet my sisters would have a ton of questions for him. About his business, about growth structure and customer base. They know all the business things that can translate across multiple platforms. All I have are books.

Hell, even my youngest sister could still keep a conversation flowing with a stranger on an eight-hour plane ride. She would ask him about his security plan for her. Where she can and cannot go. A week-

23

by-week itinerary. She'd have it edited and sent back to him to rearrange his strategy to fit her social and work life.

Shame I work from home. I work online and promote and advertise online. I interact mostly online, and hell, I even grocery shop online.

Strong coffee aromas fill the air. 'Is someone making fresh coffee?' I ask.

'Monique disappeared through the back when you woke up. Guess she's psychic with who needs what.'

'Guess you'd have to be to work on a Wembridge, Lewis, and Knight private plane,' I say.

'What does that mean?' He looks up from his phone, waiting for an answer.

'The private industry can be brutal. I can imagine the Wembridge clan is pretty demanding with their staff. You don't get to climb that high in show business without having a power ego.'

'That's an interesting perspective to take on people you've never met. Can't imagine your father gossiping about his TV carrier like that?'

I shake my head. 'He's never said anything like that. Forget it. I'm shooting my mouth off. Just, you know—Wembridge Studios makes loads of TV. Mike Knight is a twenty-million-dollar a movie man and has a million kids he flies around when he's on location, and Stella Lewis—she must really be some piece of work to represent the two of them. I heard she divorced David Wembridge and made him buy her two new houses in Beverly Hills so she could monitor his bachelor behaviour—didn't want it affecting her paycheck.' I wiggle my eyebrows, looking for some reaction to the gossip, but I get nothing. 'Apparently, they only got back together a few years ago to take the heat off that car wreck the Knights were in.'

Max picks up his phone again. 'Well, as long as that's your official stance on successful people as a stereotype. I'll remember my place as one of the hired help and only come out if you need me.'

'I'm an author. Gossip and celeb conspiracies are how I get a lot of my ideas. My *own* life is pretty boring,' I tell him. 'There's not much you're going to have to do with me.'

Max locks the screen on his phone this time and puts it away. 'I looked over your online activities and your schedule. Not much to worry about on the day-to-day. If you can let me know before any dates you have, I'm going to have to look the guy up, and the location of the date. And I need names of your book club members.'

My face drops. Hell, even my father doesn't enquire about who I date. 'Excuse me?' I squeak.

'Online dating apps and book club. It's the only things you really leave the house for.'

Oh my god. He's been inside my computer, or my social media or fuck, how the hell does he know about my Tinder dates?

Fuck fuck fuck.

'Yes, my IT guy accessed all your apps. We've deleted your Tinder profile. That one was just too much of a security risk. But he secured you a new profile, used the same picture, but skewed the photo some and changed the recognisable details.'

At least his tight smile looks a little remorseful.

'Dating preferences were all set the same. He's turned the location and check-in options off on all social media. Don't reactivate them, or we'll lock you out completely.'

'Running club.' I try to make my life sound more exciting, but I think I've failed when he looks blankly at me.

'I go running twice a week with a local club. You're going to need all their names too, right?' I nod at myself and put all of my anxieties into my work.

My fingers fly over the keys and I waste away some more hours of the day getting absorbed into a fictional world of my own. Six thousand words later, and I need a mental break. I open up my Facebook group for my readers and structure a post to auto-send when we land. My readers give me such a boost when I'm feeling low or need some adrenaline-fueled motivation to keep me writing to the end.

Hey, girls and guys. I have a quick poll for you for something new that might come soon. There might be a new support character hanging around this new idea.

25

Hot American soldier turned security guy with a serious, sexy scowl.

What direction should I send him in?

Click the options to vote below.

- Screw
- Marry
- Kill

Can't wait to see what the top votes are. Something tells me my readers are going to choose the top one. I chuckle and switch back to my writing document.

When Monique clears away our garbage and gives me a fresh bottle of water, she tells Max it's forty-five minutes till landing.

I don't speak; I type faster. I have about twenty minutes before they're going to make me turn off my laptop. I switch documents from writing to chapter plotting and fill in every thought that's going through my head. I can get the basics of scenes and chapters filed for later and flesh out tonight before I crumble in my bed.

Packing up my things on the plane, Max and I are both ready to depart with minimum fuss. I like the fact that he travels light. Anytime I've gone on family vacations, even the act of getting off the plane was fraught with packing and organising shit that'd been discarded over the flight. Makeup and phone chargers are normally in places you would never expect to find them. And my nieces and nephews' toys and shoes can never be found for at least fifteen minutes. The chaos at the start of a family vacation is just not worth it.

As the plane comes into Dublin, I look out at the view and my heart kicks up. On the right window, green fields of varying shades can be seen for miles. The other side views of houses and apartment buildings. Some close together, others spaced out on land and gardens separating the borders. The beach stretches for miles, interrupted by patches of water and hills before the sand reclaims patches of the shore. As the airport comes into view, and the roads and traffic take centre stage, I rest my head back in the seat. The plane touches Irish soil. I smile. I'm excited to be home. To get to my own house, with my own things and my own quiet space. Then I remember Max and my eyes flutter open. Shit, Max is going to invade my quiet space and my highly organised things.

'My car's parked.'

Max carries both our bags off the plane. At the bottom of the stairs, I try to take my bag out of his hand, but he holds his grip.

'I've got it.' He nods for me to keep walking in front of him.

'It's not heavy. Surely you need to have a free hand at least, to keep potential stalkers away from me, right?'

'Fine.' Max thrusts the bag out and I reach for it. 'I was being polite,' he says. 'But you're right. I really should let someone else carry the bags.' He takes the strap of his own hold-all off his shoulder and hands it to me too.

I take it from his hand, but it immediately drops to the ground. 'Damn, that didn't look heavy,' I say. 'How much stuff do you have in here?'

He shrugs. 'Six months' worth.'

Two men standing by a Merc on the tarmac approach us and introduce themselves to Max, who has stepped in front of me. They take the bags and Max leads me to the car that drives us the short distance to the part of the terminal that has Garda Passport control. Once through the queue and cleared, we're ushered through the tight hallway, through the baggage claim and customs and out to arrivals.

'Coffee would be good,' I point to the coffee stand in arrival and the men follow me over while I place an order for me and Max.

The chill oozing around the automatic doors hits my legs, and I wish I had on one of those floor-length blankets wrapped around me. The two cups of coffee in a grey cardboard carrier are steaming heat on my hands as we make the short walk over the road to the car park.

I locate my Tesla Model S on the second floor. My father splurged on my birthday gift three years ago on his last visit. He chose well. Something he knew I secretly loved and wouldn't refuse. The dark grey exterior contrasts the light white leather interior. No matter where I have to go, it always puts me in a good mood to drive there.

War and books

This year's gift was an impromptu visit home, which I thought was going to involve quality family time. Instead, I got a pile of anxiety about threats that have nothing to do with me and a security guard for half a year. They didn't even write me a card.

The dull grey of the morning isn't shedding any light or happiness through the parking lot, and it reminds me to activate the heating at home from my cell.

Max packs the trunk and I hop into the driver's seat and turn on the ignition, then push the temperature on the heated seats to high. I leave the passenger seat at a medium setting. Don't want to burn Max's ass when he gets in, and apparently those heated seats aren't good for men's sperm count. See, sometimes I can have internal thoughts and not verbalise them.

The airport staff leave Max, and he hesitates at the rear of the car, finally coming to the passenger side.

'I'd prefer to drive.' He slams the door shut and gets his belt. 'But my car is being delivered to your house this afternoon. I guess I can wait until then.'

I put the car into drive and move out of the space, slowly navigating around the tight car park.

'Can you drive a stick? Most cars are manual here, unless you've specifically asked for automatic.'

Max nods. 'My father's English. Made sure I could drive both. I have family in Dublin too. I've been here a couple of times, so I'm familiar with the north side.'

'Ah, ever driven on the left, though?'

Max looks at me. 'Have you?' He nods out the windshield, and I panic and check the road to see what side I'm driving on.

'Not funny, dude.'

Max laughs and his smile is panty-dropping, book-worthy. I shake the fog from my head. It always takes me an hour or so to get out of fantasy world after a writing sprint, and if there is someone going to be hanging around me full-time, I need to figure out how to stop the witty, sexy comments inside my head.

'So, first stop is the shopping centre down the road.' I point to the sign for Swords town to the left of the airport. 'We can pick up things you need there before we head home.'

'I don't need anything,' Max tells me.

'Actually, you do. The cottage at my house is used for storage, so although technically it's another house, it's empty. You need a bed and a couch. And a wardrobe.' I move to the left filter lane and check the oncoming traffic. 'There's a bathroom plumbed up, but no laundry or kitchen, so you'll have to use those in my house.'

My phone rings over the Bluetooth speaker. My assistant's name, Ailish, appears on the radio dashboard and I flick the call to answer.

'I'll try to stay out of your way,' Max whispers as my call connects.

'Hi, Ailish, I'm not long off the plane,' I tell her.

'Thank god, Orchid. I've been trying to ring you for hours.'

I look at my watch and it's only 8:30 am. 'Why have you been awake for hours?'

'Your pre-order got cancelled.' She breathes down the phone. 'I needed to check if it was you before I called the online team and kicked up a shitstorm.'

'Of course it wasn't me.' I shriek. 'Are you sure it's cancelled?'

I can hear some paperwork being moved around as Ailish answers. 'I got an email refunding my order and when I checked your author account, it's been cancelled. It's the biggest sales platform, Orchid. It took us months to promote and build those sales. We don't have enough time to do it again.'

Ailish sounds as stressed as my heart feels. Release day is the biggest day for book launches. It's where I'll make any sort of income off the book and set up for any online awards or categories.

'Okay, speak to the support services and see what happened. This has to be a glitch on their end. It's only us and the web team that have access to the author platform, and our sign-ins are secure. Then get the web team to open up pre-orders on our site again and send out as SOS newsletter and social media posts. If we act now, we might claw some of them back. And set up a live feed for me later tonight so I can tell my reader groups what happened.'

'I'm sorry,' Ailish says.

She's devastated, like me. She works hard on every release that we do, and she feels like she's failed. 'Let's just sort it out. I'll be at home later. Call me and we can catch up with progress.' I keep driving to the store to order Max furniture, not thinking about the hundreds of thousands of dollars I've probably lost.

'We should get you a fridge for out there too,' I say to Max. 'I have a handyman who might hook up a stove or whatever. I need to call him.'

I like deflection. There's no need pondering over the shit I can't control. I have people working on the problem for me, and I need to calm my racing headspace.

'I can survive with whatever you have already.' Max looks at me from the corner of his eyes. He must know that this is serious, but it's also none of his business, so I like that he's not asking questions.

'In that case, you can always boil a kettle for ramen noodles, although you look like you eat more protein than that.'

Max shifts in his seat. Fuck. I've made him uncomfortable again. I say inappropriate things, and people always take it the wrong way. Although it's not inappropriate, it's just incomplete. I stop myself from saying the entirety of what I'm thinking, and that ends up being worse.

I feel bad. He's uprooted his life to come on this job and he doesn't even have a clear nine-to-five work pattern to claim the evenings to himself and his friends.

'You leave a girlfriend at home?' I ask.

Max looks at me and shakes his head before turning back to watch the road.

'Sorry, just wondering what you're going to do in your spare time here.'

'I won't have spare time. I'm going to be on you.'

'On me?'

'Trailing you. Wherever you go, I go.'

'I don't go to many places, as you already know.' I circle the roundabout and turn right to a furniture shop off the main road. 'The shopping centre is just down the road for when we're finished here. We need sheets and lighting and towels. You probably want toiletries too. We can get you a TV. You might be bored out there longer than you realise. We can get groceries in the store next to my place.'

It takes less than an hour to order furniture. Neither Max nor I attempt to look around the shop. Once the sales assistant approaches us at the door, I list off items of furniture and soft furnishings I need and the colour scheme I have on the walls and flooring. I add in crockery, electrical goods, and small appliances, and I just hope that my handyman can hook up some sort of basic cooking facilities on the small workspace that's already in place in the kitchen.

I explain to the sales assistant I want whatever he could have delivered and assembled before closing today.

'You don't have to get everything. A bed would be fine.' Max is pacing behind me.

I enter my pin on the keypad and keep my back turned when I lie. 'It's about time I set up the cottage for guests.'

No one visits me, not really.

On the drive home, I point out to Max the various routes that can take us back to my place and the exit for the motorway that I avoid and stay on the old roads. The village of Lusk is twenty minutes from the airport and less than that from where we shopped.

I take him past my house on the main back road and through the village to the supermarket to get supplies before I hide away for a few days.

Max twists in his seat as we drive past my property. 'Isn't that your place?'

'How the hell do you know?'

'I've seen the plans, some pictures. Locating it on the map wasn't hard. The old real estate pictures were still online from when you bought it. Were buried deep in Google search, but I've had them removed now.'

'Jesus, really?'

Max nods. 'Home layout, doors and window count. Property size and dimensions distance from main road and routes to the

31

motorway for a quick escape. It's scary how the internet can be misused.'

'Wow, thank you.' I look at him across the central divide. 'I never would have thought to even look to see if that was still online.'

'Shop's parking lot is closed in, narrow entrance and exit, and a pedestrian crossing. Not a good road to get out of quickly. I'd suggest parking out front instead.'

I look at the road, where we can't see the shop from here. 'You looked up my local amenities?'

'Amongst other things.'

My frustrations are with the need to invade my life, rather than the guy who is just getting paid to be here.

'This entire ordeal is nothing to even do with me. It's all because of careers my family chose over a relationship with me. And I might still pay the price for it.'

'All families have a dynamic of sorts, Orchid. Sometimes it's their health or personalities that you have to make allowances for invading your life. For other people, it's their career that imposes upon you.'

I shake my head and rest my elbow on the edge of the door. There's no way to understand living on the outskirts of a Hollywood life. To know what that kind of money and fame can do to a family. To see how other people react, both good and bad.

'Your family isn't the centre of attention,' I tell him. 'Your family doesn't attract psychos who might ever leave behind recording devices to sell to the newspapers. Your family isn't the target of huge financial robberies.'

It's a fear I've had for a while. One that's materialising. My sisters especially don't realise how vulnerable they've been leaving themselves. Almost whoring out their lives and locations over social media, in the guise of sharing their lives and consumer habits, for the possibility of selling more of their sponsored products.

chapter four

Orchid

'Nice house,' Max says when I turn into the driveway.

Although the property is technically facing a busy main road, it's still quiet.

'Space and the quiet were more desirable for me than location to a busy city.' I park on the gravel drive and get out.

Lusk itself is a small town almost an hour outside of Dublin. So the contrast from living here on two acres of land, compared to LA, is vast.

Once Max joins me, he looks behind him. 'It's easily accessible and visible from the main road.'

'Never had the need for added security before.' The irritation under my skin is back and prickling around my body again. There was a reason I wanted separation from the public life my family sought like a drug. And their drama that they make a career of has now infiltrated my sanctuary.

'We need to install gates,' he says.

'I have gates.' I look at the entrance.

Max shakes his head. 'No, you have a fence.' He takes my hand and tugs me the fifty yards from my front door to the fence and the two-foot patch of grass that separates the main road. 'A fence that comes up to your waist. Hell, I bet you could jump this in a hurdle race.'

'Guess I could try that the next time I have a party.' I shrug. I never have parties.

'Your father already allocated me a budget for anything that needs to be upgraded. I've ordered a five-foot perimeter gate to run the full length of the property divide along the road. We're going to install smaller fencing to separate the back of the property from the neighbours. An electric gate should go up front, a closed wooden one so people can't see in. I've placed an order, but you can choose the finishing ascetics. And if you're planning on staying here for twenty years—I'd get some mature trees and hedging running along the inside of the perimeter. Helps with privacy, but also for people not being able to jump the fence as easily. Maybe some hawthorn so people can't come in without getting scratched the hell up. We can install electric current wires through the hedging. This close to farms, we can use the premise that it's keeping the animals in the correct fields.'

I shrug, not committing to agreeing or arguing with Max. I'm tired and I don't want to end our first day together fighting.

Max walks to the front door and inspects the mail box screwed to the wall.

'This needs to be moved to the gate. I'll have them install it so the mailman doesn't need to come up here.'

'He needs to come up here. I get a lot of parcel deliveries. He normally drives the van right in here.'

'Fine. Mailman I'll get on board with. Everyone else, cold sales and junk mail aren't getting through the gate. There's a new security monitoring company coming to hook up cameras and alarm codes.' Max checks his watch. 'Should be here in two hours. I need to see the rest of the property, then inside before they get here.'

I groan. 'This is it,' I tell him. 'House, original cottage that you are now taking over. No garage, open space garden.' I turn on my heel. 'Road.' I point. 'I need food, a shower, and a nap and I also want to clear all my stuff out of the cottage and bring it into the spare office I have upstairs. And I'm going to do it in that order.'

I open the door and rummage through the drawers in the hallway table, looking for the key to the cottage. When I turn around, Max is leaning on the doorjamb.

'You're not a vampire, are you?'

He smirks and takes a step inside. 'You don't write paranormal romance,' he says.

I scoff. 'How the hell do you know?' For all he knows, I could be the EL James of the vampire world.

'You left the country for four days and never set your alarms.'

I look up at the alarm keypad on the inside of the door, like it's going to tell Max that he's wrong. That I really punched in a key to disarm the alarms when I opened the door. But I know I never set it. I was in a hurry when I left and had to go back inside three times for things I forgot. My phone charger, my printed chapter notes for the new novel I'm working on, and the bag of Irish chocolates I got my dad for his office. It surprises even me I don't keep better security of my house. My work and office should be more of a security priority for me.

'It won't happen again,' I tell him.

I show Max around the house. It doesn't take long.

The house has three bedrooms, small by my parents' standards, but otherwise it's a pretty decent size house. More than enough for me and, more importantly, I bought it myself. With my own earnings and cleared the mortgage in five years.

I still do a little victory dance inside my head each time I think about that.

Half a million euros is a decent amount to earn by the time you're twenty-three. Granted, I had earned some of that when I started writing in LA. I still lived at home, in the guesthouse, avoiding everything remotely reality TV from the main house, and wrote in my Batcave alone.

But when I was eighteen and wanted to write a book about Ireland, I was old enough to pack up my things, cash in my savings, and buy a house online.

I knew I wasn't coming here to research one book. I was coming here because it was my dream location to live. The lifestyle contrast and landscape were the serenity I wanted to live my life by, no matter how stupid it was to buy a house I'd only seen photos of.

Fifty percent deposit on a home, and a shipping container of all my belongings.

I paid the rest of the house off as quickly as I could. No unnecessary spending. No new clothes or travel back home. No vacations or even heavy splurges in the supermarket.

I wrote and released novels like a bitch on heat those first couple of years here. Mixed traditional publishing with self-publishing to fill the gaps of release buzz, and I jumped up and down when I made the last payment on the house.

I could take the pressure off myself, but by that time I had my creating, writing, and promotional work down to a fine art. The writing and releasing and earning continued.

'Guest bedroom is on the right.' I point to the door that is behind him. 'But it doesn't get used much. Living room is next door.' I tap the door as we pass. 'There's a fireplace in there, so I work in that room in the winter evenings.'

Max puts his head around the door. It's big enough for the overly large couch and a wall full of installed book shelves.

The TV is screwed to the wall. It's only used when I need to rest and binge on mindless distractions.

'Kitchen, utility, and office are out here.' When you walk from the hallway to the kitchen, the entire back wall is glass, looking out to the field I own. It backs up to the neighbouring farmland and rolling hills, and a road in the distance. You can see some cars driving along, but they are far enough away you can't even hear them when you are sitting out on the deck.

'I spend most of my time in this part of the house.' I sit at the dinner table in the kitchen and let Max look around the most intimate part of my life—my work. 'To look out and get lost in a view is a major relaxation saviour when things become too much.'

The official dining room's been converted into my office. A designer picked out functional but relaxing and comfortable furniture, and colour tones that won't distract or overwhelm me. I knocked out the wall to have the open plan from the kitchen and installed a push back, barn style door, so that if there ever were people here, I could close off my workspace.

It's usually open so I can have easy access to coffee and grab sandwiches when I need to fuel myself in a writing marathon.

Max walks over and I'm glad I love a tidy workspace and thank the lord for a junk drawer that the random pens and lists get thrown into. A large desk, with printer, paper, coloured pens and highlighters, my computer, and laptop are lined up. I transfer all my notes onto the main computer at the end of the day, as I'll do with the mini travel laptop I had with me in LA this week.

Printed copies of manuscripts in the making are filed in boxes on the walls, with folders of notes. Purchase orders and swag manufacturers have their own shelf. Tax and accountancy documents, seller accounts and contracts and delivery notes have a filing cabinet. Orders placed and awaiting delivery have a shelf, as do returns and outgoing tracking numbers.

I smile at Max and want someone to be impressed with my organisation, but I also want him to turn around and see the view.

Max shrugs out of his jacket. 'You said you wanted boxes moved into the office?'

I point up. 'They need to be stored in the upstairs office. I won't have space here—but I have them labelled and in order, so you're going to have to move the boxes I tell you and help me get them back in the corresponding place when I figure it out upstairs.'

Max's eyes widen at me. 'Okay,' he says.

'I'm not weird,' I tell him. 'I have a lot of inventory. I need a system, like any good mini warehouse operating out of a spare room would be.'

'Okay,' he says.

'Why don't you look around and unpack the groceries from the car. I'll start moving the furniture around upstairs. Hopefully, we'll be finished by tonight.'

'Okay.'

I stop and wait for him to say anything else. 'Do you normally keep conversation to a minimum, or have I pissed you off?'

'Lucky for you, I have a high tolerance.' His eyes narrow slightly, but there is more disappointment than anger.

37

Fuck—this happens all the time. People let inappropriate comments slide, and then once they have time to think about it, they realise they should have been pissed off. I wonder which one pushed him over the edge?

Max is walking around the outside of the house when my phone dings. I realise I've gravitated to the window to get a look at him while I check my message.

Only it's a Tinder notification on my new account that was set up.

Great, I wonder what people I'm going to match with now that Max has had his IT guy in my account.

Hmm, not as disappointing as I thought. Mostly my profile looks the same, and my previous messages are all still there.

Christ, I hope they didn't read them. It's not my fault I get sent dick pics, and in fairness, I only follow through with those dates if I was already committed to a time and place on my calendar.

New guy who was texting last week has sent another message to see if I'm back in town yet. Might as well plan a date when I still have some hold over my social life.

I type out a message about dinner on Saturday, and I get a reply straight away. Eight o'clock in Fire, Dublin. Nice. I normally hate driving into Dublin at night, but if Maxy boy is going to be chaperoning everything from now on, I can push myself out of my comfort zone and meet more people.

I peer down the window at Max. What the hell is he taking notes on? He better not be reporting back to my father like I'm some little girl who needs daddy's approval on how I live my life in my home.

Now that he has his jacket off, his muscular arms are on show through the snug-fitting fabric as his arms flex while he writes. He really could be an inspiration for my next novel. Max the super-hot security guard. I wonder if he needs to tie someone up or if he could restrain them with his sexy, silent stare. I should check my Facebook feed and see how the voting is going on the new poll.

I flick the pages over and smile at the *Screw* voting numbers.

I giggle and know I have to cut it out. Most people don't live in a world of creating romance plot lines in their day-to-day life. Most people don't live with their heads permanently in the gutter.

I've already said inappropriate things to him and I need to remember he's not one of my readers in the private group where we talk about which characters we love or who our favourite book boyfriends are.

Max is real, and he's here for work. And fuck—he's looking at me, staring at him.

I wave.

Why the fuck do I wave?

It's not like I could duck and cover and pretend I wasn't looking at him.

Max raises his hand and, with one sharp movement that could only be described as awkward, waves back.

Shit, this is not good.

Operation *write Max as a baddy* is going to have to commence. I flick back to my Facebook private page and break the news in my readers' group. But I can't log in. Shit—my account has been locked. I read the pop-up message that explains I have a temporary ban for posting *Inappropriate content.* I'm supposed to go into social and beg my readers to repurchase my book. Fuck.

chapter five

Orchid

I call Ailish and trot down the stairs to the front door as the phone is ringing.

'Are you locked out of Facebook?' she asks as soon as she answers the call.

'Yes,' I tell her. 'How did you know?'

'Because I am too.'

'For fuck's sake, Ailish, we're the only admins on the page. How are we going to run it?'

'Don't worry, I called my sister and got her log in details. She said you can go into the group as her and post your video from her account. We're still on other platforms, so no panic. I'm sorting everything out from here.'

'Okay.' I sigh. 'I'm sending you a box of wine when today is over, okay?'

'Make sure it's a nice one.' I can hear the smile in Ailish's voice.

Max has made his way around the side of the house and is waiting in the driveway for me. I hang up my call and open up the cottage door and walk in.

'What the fuck?' Max drawls from the entrance of the cottage.

I'm standing at my front door, which is less than ten feet from the cottage entrance, and I can't help but chuckle. 'Told you I needed time for a system,' I shout out like I would if I were a child teasing my brother.

Max turns and shakes his head at me, hiding the grin that's tugging at his mouth.

From the outside, the cottage looks small, but it's big enough for an open plan living and kitchen space. Two double bedrooms and a full bathroom are at the back.

The space is currently filled with rows of boxes ranging from one foot to four feet high, stacked along the walls.

I have sheets of paper taped to the walls, labelling up imaginary aisles.

Boxes of paperback books that are self-published and available for online signing and sales in one place—organised by series and title.

Thirteen books and novellas mean thirteen different rows of boxes from the printers.

Traditionally published books for giveaways and charity donations and raffles.

Traditionally published copies that are for sale have to be kept separate. As an approved distributor of my work, I technically don't own these.

Marketing material ranging from signage to be seen from the side of the road to bookmarks and posters to display around local events.

Book related products like emblazed mugs, stress balls, pens and notepads, jewellery, candy, and clothing are organised by product, size, and sub categorised into those for sale, or those for giveaways at events.

'Most of them are heavy, so we're going to be a while.' I move inside with him. 'We should start with the smaller ones up front here. We can lay them out as a mirror image upstairs. I have an assistant that comes once a week to help me fill orders, so she needs to know where everything is as usual.

'The real hard work will be to haul those boxes in the back. They're all full of books. They need to be stacked against the walls. Get them in a similar layout in the upstairs office.' I point over my shoulder. 'I have some book shelves up there already that you're going to have to help me move into my bedroom first. I've already taken the books out—so I just need some of your muscle.' I cringe inside when I say it.

'We'll get started before the furniture delivery and security guys get here.' Max pushes up his shirt sleeves that were already a little tight on him, and I roll my eyes.

It takes two hours, and Max has to pay the security guys to help us haul the last of the boxes upstairs. It's official. My family has turned my life upside down. Which is impressive since there is an ocean separating us.

I spend another hour organising it the way I want while Max and the others move around the house like I'm not here, like I don't even own the place.

But I actually like my stock being up here. I've never had the chance or the help to move everything in one go. I think I'm going to get the delivery guys to help me set them upstairs every week from now on. Beats going out to the cottage to fill orders and take stock, especially when it pours rain unexpectedly.

I stand back and admire our work, while Max talks shop downstairs.

It's the first time I've not spent all day obsessing over writing, but it was fun having someone to chat to while I pottered around the house.

Max isn't chatty much, but he listened as I told him all about my plans for the London book signing event for Halloween and all the giveaway swag I'm planning on having custom-made for the event.

I flip the switch for the hot water as the furniture guys arrive and I run downstairs to direct them where to set up.

After showering, I'm back and forth making coffee for everyone. Before I know it, I've turned into the perfect host and am making sandwiches for the furniture installers as they build and place everything we bought this morning.

I lay out a plate of food and cookies for Max and the security guys at the dining table, as they finish up their recap of camera installations and procedures and show Max the range of each camera in real time.

I still need to talk to Max about what he can and cannot do while he's living here, but want to wait until he's on his own.

I fidget in the living room, moving some books around the coffee table, and then realise I need to clean under the sofa. Once the place is spotless, I flop onto the couch in the living room, while I wait for Max to finish up with the vast amount of people who have trawled through my house today.

I do something I don't normally do until late in the evening. I turn on the TV.

Sometimes I can't help myself flipping to the WReality! channel and seeing what show is on. It's like a morbid torture of family life.

I can't watch a full episode. That's like an entire hour documentary about how I'm no longer a part of their life.

But the trailers are good.

My brothers and sisters are normally fighting over something, and my mom is usually flipping the bird at someone who won't do as they're told. It makes me want to call them, be a part of their crazy life for a second each day.

Max knocks on the door and I jump from the couch.

I tilt my head around the side of the door, and he is waiting in the hallway for me.

'You can come in, you know.'

'It's your space. I'm not going to move around the place like I live here. I told you I'd try to stay out of your way.'

I let out a long sigh. 'Is everyone all done rearranging my home?'

'I'm happy with the progress today.'

Max ignores my jibe, so I decide to be brass with him too.

'I don't have a housekeeper.' I sit on the edge of the couch opposite the living room door. 'So you're going to have to tidy up after yourself and do your own laundry. I have a cleaner that comes in once a week. I'll ask her to add the cottage onto her list. She doesn't tidy or put away your things. She's just going to clean.'

Max nods. 'That's not a problem. I need her schedule, too.'

43

'Mondays. Everything around here happens on a Monday. Groceries get delivered, cleaner comes, assistant comes, and any jobs I have for the handyman get scheduled on a Monday. It's the only day I take off, so there're no interruptions to my work time. It's also the only day I cook for the week, so if you want anything, let me know by Sunday so I can order the ingredients. There're individual portions of food in the freezer. All you need to do is reheat, but let me know what you take so I can adjust my menu plan.'

'Anything else?'

'I need you to be quick when you're in the kitchen. I get distracted easily by movements, and that's my workspace. If you can make your meals or whatever and clear out of here, I'd appreciate that. You can use this room if you need to be in the main house.'

'That'll work for me.'

'The gym is in the second bedroom in the cottage, so unfortunately I'll be coming out there three times a week to invade a bit of your space. I hope that's okay.'

'Of course it's okay.'

'I—' Shit, why is this so hard to say? 'I don't want you in the house at night. Once it gets dark, I lock the place up, and I don't want to have people in and out the door if it's unnecessary.'

'I told you I won't get in the way. I'll need to do a sweep of the house before you lock up, but that'll be it. I'll keep watch on the perimeter, and we can talk on the phone or the alarm.' Max hands me a small key-fob with a red button on it.

'Keep this on you at all times. It's connected to me, the security company, and the Gardai, so everyone will be alerted. You've been placed on the high response list because of the recent incidents your family has experienced. This one'—he gives me a small walkie-talkie—'is if you want to speak to just me.'

'I have a phone, you know.'

'I know, but signals and connection times can be temperamental when you need them. I set up a charger station at the side of your bed, so make sure the walkie's housed there at night. There's another charging port in your office in case the battery runs low during the day. This way, we have every option.'

The TV catches my attention behind me when I hear my family name being used with the attention grabbing "breaking news" announcement. I'm still on the reality channel, so it's not like it's the actual news, but I turn around and see a picture of my family home on the screen.

I scan the words on the red banner running at the bottom of the screen that say *Gun threat at Rock Family Home,* but switch my attention to the information the host of the show is spouting off.

Max has pulled out his phone and is talking as he walks into the kitchen. 'Why wasn't I alerted to this sooner?' I hear him from the other room.

'Information is still unclear, but sources can confirm that at least two people were arrested on the Rock property who were armed...'

'Everyone's okay,' Max tells me from the doorway and I hear my phone ringing from the office.

I run into the other room, knowing that my brief span of a ringer will cut out and send the caller to voicemail before I get there. The screen says seven missed calls from my dad.

I call him back and he tells me the little information he knows about what happened. The security guys caught two men on the property. They'd already entered the guesthouse at the far end of the pool and were making their way over to the main house when they were apprehended. 'They didn't spend much time in the guesthouse,' Dad tells me and his voice cracks at the end. 'The team here think they were looking for a person for some sort of hostage situation, or to force us to transfer money or open the safe. If they were looking for things to steal, they would have tossed the guesthouse over, even a little.'

'It's okay, Dad,' I tell him. 'No one got hurt. You have a great team there.'

'You would have been the first person they got,' my dad whispers on the phone. 'If you'd moved back home like we asked you—or had you stayed a little longer like we begged for you to be

45

close by while this threat was taken care of, you'd have been out there by yourself. They would have got you.'

'I'm not there, Dad. They weren't after me. They were after money. I'm far away from all the drama, and no one even knows who I am here. Don't forget, I have your crazy security team extending all the way over here now. Max has already secured things up here.' I look at Max, who nods at me. 'He's here if you want to talk to him. Let you know that I'm all safe.'

I pass the phone over to Max and sit in my office chair while Max reassures my father that I'm safe five thousand miles away in a remote house on my own.

I might not be a part of the *Rock Family Drama* TV show, but my parents are wealthy and someone just tried to rob them. My siblings make enough money put together to be able to run a small country. Like it or not, I could be a part of that financial target.

Maybe Max and his little security upgrades and the reassurance that brings just turned out to be worth every favour and penny my dad paid.

chapter six

Orchid

It's only taken four weeks for Max and me to fall into a comfortable routine.

Eight a.m. and my alarm sounds at the side of my bed.

A groan from behind me, and a strong arm snakes around my stomach. Instead of squeezing me in for a hug, he reaches over and silences the alarm and rolls over.

Whatever.

'I need you to get up.' I throw the blanket off the bed and the naked man on the bed's not happy with me.

My phone rings on the nightstand and I smile when Max's name flashes on the screen.

I swipe the call button and he doesn't even wait for a greeting.

'Breakfast is ready, Molly.'

How the hell does he know I put him on speakerphone? He's never once in the month got confused and called me my real name in front of anyone. Although he's never called me anything but Orchid when we're alone. I would have thought he would have just saved himself the trouble and called me Molly the whole time. It's what I'm used to here; no one really getting the distinction that there are two parts to me, to my life.

'Ugh.' I sigh heavily with thanks. 'I'll be right down.'

Hanging up the call, I gather the clothes on the ground and throw them at Archie. 'Time to go home.'

'Don't I get breakfast too?' he asks.

'Sorry, I have a full day.'

'It's Saturday.' He turns his nose up at me as he pulls his pants on.

'I work Saturdays. You know that.'

I have my workout gear on and run down the stairs with Archie on my heel as I pull my hair off my neck and tie it up.

At the bottom of the stairs, I open the front door. I don't even need him to walk through the house.

He kisses me on the cheek, but something behind me catches his eye and I know he can see Max in the kitchen.

Speaking louder than he needs to, Archie says, 'I've booked dinner tonight. You be ready for nine?'

Two dates in one week are too much for me, but I'm throwing a guy out the morning after sex, and I want to hold onto a bit of morals.

'Sure,' I agree. 'I'll change some things around today to make sure I finish work early.'

'I'll collect you at eight thirty then?'

I shake my head. 'I'll have Max drive me.'

I prefer Max's car anyway, even to mine. It's fast and spacious, and the height of the four-by-four makes the journey of the road feel safer somehow. And I can write in his car without getting a headache.

'Text the restaurant details, and I'll meet you there.'

It means I can wrap up any emails or admin work in the car on the way over without feeling bad that I should talk to him. Max never makes me feel bad for finishing up the working day rather than making small talk.

With downcast eyes, Archie leaves the house and I don't mean to slam the door, but it slips out of my hand and closes more forcefully than I intended.

As I pass the living room, Max's laptop is open, and he has a pile of notes on the side of the couch.

The his-and-her offices next door to each other have worked well.

That man works more than I do, and we don't interrupt each other.

Although I think he stops to listen to me when I do live video feeds in my reader groups.

There's always a silence that goes back to the regular tapping of a keyboard once I'm done.

Max has already used the time I spent holed up here to double job and work on growing and managing his business. I'm impressed. It would be easy to take this gig as the straightforward job that it is, sit back and enjoy the rest while getting paid. But he's taken the opportunity to not only help himself out in the future, but to get my ass into better shape.

We were only back in Dublin for one night when there was an altercation at a book singing and Max insisted I start self-defence training with him.

It really wasn't as dramatic as it sounds. I went outside to get some promo photos taken in front of the bookstore and a homeless woman grabbed me. She was really only trying to get my attention for some cash, but she wouldn't let go of my arm. When Max made it to me, he got the woman off and slipped her a twenty in the process. But Max wanted me to free myself from someone's grasp quicker than waiting for help. Which only makes sense. So I've added training with Max to my workout routine.

In the kitchen, Max hands me a smoothie and keeps his eyes on his phone.

'Why does this one take so long in the driveway? He's just sitting in his car on his phone.' Max looks up at me from the security feed app on his phone. 'He has sixty more seconds before I have to go out there and eject him from the property.'

'Relax, Rambo. He's probably sorting the radio or plugging in his phone. Not everyone can hightail it out of a girl's house in under a minute.'

'Last month's Jason certainly could.' Max smirks.

I punch him in the stomach to shut him up and I know he lets me make contact with him. He's a faster mover than I'll ever be. I never get to make contact with him when we're training.

49

Max checks his phone. 'Okay, time's up.' He makes for the door, but I stop him with a moan in between swallowing down the drink.

'What the hell is in this one?'

'Just the essentials. Come on, we can throw him out together on the way to my place.'

'Great, that really makes me sound like a RL whore.'

'RL?' Max asks as he takes the glass out of my hand and rinses it under the tap.

'Real life, you know, rather than book life?'

'What's the difference?' he asks.

Through the hallway, I say, 'Everyone can be a book boyfriend whore, be in love with multiple male characters, and read the same books back and forth. It's sort of like cheating on all your lovers, in the book world, of course.'

'Of course.' Max closes and locks the door behind him.

We stare at the empty driveway, and there is a sense of relief from both of us.

'In real life, it has whole different consequences.'

'It sure does,' he mumbles as he stares at the automatic gates closing behind Archie's car that has hightailed it out of here in three minutes instead of one.

'Come on,' I tell him. 'You promised me I could kick you in the face today.'

In Max's cottage, we pass through the living space and into the back room that has all the gym equipment and training mats that Max added. He laughs at me. 'I told you, you could *try to* kick me in the face. No way are you going to manage.'

Despite our workouts taking an hour each morning, I actually work better and faster than I used to. Max has me leaner and more muscular than my jog three times a week used to leave me. Plus, his cooking skills are to die for. The food has certainly helped my training.

Lunch and dinner, he makes fresh, rather than my frozen portions. Instead of being a distraction, the smell that man makes in the kitchen has me working faster to get to the dining table with him. Because now, I actually take a thirty-minute lunch break.

Before Max has turned around, I've changed my stance and go to take a run at his back. He rotates out of place and puts his arms out to catch me in mid-rush. He shakes his head with mock disappointment. 'Stretch first. Then we're running sprints for thirty minutes. Then you get to jump me.'

'Why do you always save the best for last?'

'Isn't that what you do? Save all the good stuff for the readers towards the end?'

'How do you know?' I drop to the ground and mirror Max's leg stretches. 'You binge read romance novels out here at night now?'

'Maybe?' he says. 'Got to do something to distract me when you accidentally lean on the *talk* button on the walkie when you're with your Tinder dates.'

My face falls and I swear the smoothie crawls back up my throat and gets stuck mid-way.

Max stares at me, not moving.

'You little liar.' I laugh at him. 'That's not funny.'

He smiles, but it fades quickly. 'Yeah, it's really not.'

'Shit, Max. Damn, that's so embarrassing. And stop talking about my dates like I'm a RL whore. I've had two guys here since you've moved in. It's not the most shocking behaviour in the world.'

Max stands and pulls me with him to stretch out our arms. 'No, the most shocking thing is you think you're going to find a relationship on Tinder.'

'How else am I going to meet people? The friends I have don't like to mix in bars or clubs either, so the places I could meet someone are the library or online.'

'I'd try the library from now on. Start hanging out there more often. See how you get on.'

'Shut up, dude. What about you? When was the last time you got laid?'

Max is not happy with that comment. I know all of his expressions by now. Even when he's trying to be mad or serious with me, I always can see the laughter in his eyes, or the softness when he

51

is telling me about an incident that happened to one of my family in LA.

I should apologise. I shouldn't be inappropriate. But damn, I can't bring myself to take it back. I want him uncomfortable. I want him to see the same lines he shouldn't be crossing with my private life.

'What? You don't want me to talk about your sex life? But you think it's okay to make fun of mine?'

Max's eyes soften. The moment has passed. 'I wasn't making fun, Orchid.'

I like Max dressed in his suit. He doesn't dress formally often. It was something we agreed on early. For the day-to-day things and the occasional outings, it's never needed. But any work meetings I have, he would don the suit and look the part as my official driver and security. And when I went out on a date—he always dressed in charge.

'Nice dress.' I meet Max in the driveway and he's standing at the car, waiting to open the door for me. I don't know why I love that. Maybe because a guy has never picked me up for a date before, and I would imagine that if they did, I'd love them to be waiting to get the door for me.

'Thanks, you too.' I smile at him.

'Smart-ass.' He closes the door once I'm safely tucked inside and he gets in the driver's seat.

'You sure you're going to be warm enough tonight? The temperature's already dropping.'

'That's why it's a full-length. Keep these newly toned pins all warm,' I joke. I open my purse and before I've pulled up the email app, Max has handed me a power cord.

'Thanks,' I say. 'I need to get a new phone. This thing isn't holding a charge anymore.'

'I can get you one tomorrow if you want to pay cash. But if you want to go back on a contract, you're going to have to come sign.'

'I might just send you if that's okay?' I don't look up, but I know Max has nodded his confirmation. He knows what I like in a phone. I'm not even going to ask him to call me with specifications when he's in the shop. Everything with him is as easy as it is with my assistant, and that took two years to get there with her. Despite there being no need for a personal security guard in my life, I like having him here.

The waiter shows me to the table, and Archie isn't here yet. I'm five minutes late, so I guess I can't be mad at him for punctuality.

Max takes my coat and pulls out my chair for me while I order a glass of Sav Blanc.

'Bored already?' he asks.

'What?'

'You only drink wine when you're bored. Or when you're trying to stop yourself from working too many hours into the night.'

'Sorry, I'm late.' Archie barrels down the restaurant and gives Max a look.

Max waits for me to look at him before he eyes the corner of the restaurant. 'I'll wait over there.'

'Might as well head home. I can take it from here.' Archie puts a ten-euro note in Max's suit pocket.

A ten, really? Aren't I at least worth a twenty? I want to be worth a twenty to someone.

Max retreats to the corner of the restaurant where I can see him, and he slips the banknote into the tip jar on the bar. When he turns, he notices me watching him, and he averts his eyes.

chapter seven

Orchid

Archie is already ranting on about something. On paper, he should be dateable material. He's two years older than me, has a job that he loves, and lives in a nice town. He's tall, dark, and handsome. Attractive, and he smells nice. Wasn't too selfish in bed last night, but there was a comfort element missing. That level of intimacy when you know someone and you can relax while they're fucking you.

I know it exists; I've written about it. Readers rave about it.

Maybe it's not real, and it's the unicorn we're all chasing. Maybe I just make it up really well and that's why I've sold so many books.

I'd say a tonne, but it's more than that.

A tonne is roughly two thousand books. I worked it out one day when I was procrastinating from writing. Most of my books weigh roughly 500 grams. I know this for shipping, but I went the whole hog and got out the kitchen scale, Google, and a calculator. Two thousand books are a tonne weight.

I wonder how many Amazon trucks that would take to deliver. I'd need to take into consideration the individual packaging and space that would take. I never worked that one out.

But it is a whole load of book-boyfriend weight riding on a fake unicorn. Every woman out there is hoping it's real.

I down the first gulp of wine and know that in less than an hour, I can finish dinner, skip dessert, and thank Archie for the five dates we've had and never see him again.

Archie shifts in his seat the entire meal, like he doesn't want to be here either. He's maybe figured out he's not getting laid tonight.

When I refuse the dessert menu, Archie tries to convince me to order something, or at least share with him, but Max has already made his way over to us and helps me with my coat.

It's like he has a security bug inside my head. He always knows when I'm being polite and would really rather leave.

'Well, since you're still here, you can give us a ride home,' Archie tells Max as he pulls out his card. 'I'll settle up and meet you at the car.'

I roll my eyes and Max escorts me to the door and my shoulders relax and the tension leaves me. A date is supposed to be fun, not tense like a job interview you know you don't even want.

I don't think Max realises when his hand lands on the small of my back, guiding me out of the door. 'You bringing him home?' Max asks.

'Hell no, we can drop him in Malahide on the way.'

Max chuckles. 'I'll leave the bad news for you to deliver.'

'Don't worry, I'm just going to say something like, *Sorry, must dash*,' I mock.

Outside at the car, Max opens the door. 'What's with the English accent?'

'Don't know.' I shrug from the back seat as Max takes his place upfront. 'I'm writing about an English couple, and sometimes it slips out.'

He shakes his head. 'That's weird. You have conversations in your head with people that aren't real. And the accent sucked. My dad doesn't sound one bit like that.'

'Why did he move to the States?' I lean forward and rest my head on the back of the passenger seat.

'He went to college in LA, and then got some work after he met my mom. Never thought to leave when they split up.'

'He's not army like you?'

Max shakes his head and turns the heater up for me. 'Nah, he did a lot of different things when I was growing up. Sometimes he and my mom work together if their jobs line up, and I liked that as a kid because he was around every day.'

'My dad's never around.' The two glasses of wine are allowing my real thoughts to slip out.

'Well, you live across an ocean.'

55

'I moved across an ocean to make it feel like the distance was something that stopped us from seeing each other. Even when I lived in the house, or when I was seventeen and moved into the guesthouse, I never saw my parents much. It's the problem with being raised in a rich family. You get bought everything you ever want, but you don't get to have a family.'

'If you say so.'

'What? You think I'm being ungrateful? That I don't know the struggles your mom must have had on her own once your parents were divorced? I know you still send money home to her, so I get I should be grateful for what I have.'

Max turns to me. 'I don't send money home to my mother, Orchid. What gave you that idea?'

'I heard you arguing with the bank one day. That you transferred money that she needed.'

Max laughs. 'That's your problem, Orchid, you're so busy putting labels on people in your books, catering to the old stereotypes and tropes, that you don't even see what's right in front of you.'

'And what's that?'

'People have all kinds of lives. We don't need to be boxed into one category. Just because my mom was divorced twenty years ago, doesn't mean she still needs her grown son to pay her bills. Just because I'm a soldier turned security guy, doesn't mean I'm down on my luck.'

'I never said that,' I shriek.

'But you think it.' He shakes his head. 'And while we're at it. I don't think you can label the way people parent their children, based on how much money they have. Some people that are rich are the best parents. And some people that have nothing are the best parents. Maybe your parents just suck, regardless of their income level. Although I don't think that's true.'

I scoff. 'You don't know them.' I wait a beat before I continue. 'You want to know the worst thing about me? I'm turning into them. I tried to run away, to rebel and have a career in the arts—something that was going to take up too much time and effort and never produce much money. Something to show them I could live with the basics and still be happy. Guess what, I fucked up and my career rocketed. And now I'm just as miserable as I've always been.'

'Poor little rich kid, Orchid,' he teases. 'You hate your money so much, why don't you give it away? There're plenty of people, charities, that will all take it from you.'

I know. But I earned it. And even though I hate myself for it, I'm proud of what I've achieved. 'Deep down I know it's not the money. It's me who's broken.'

The back door opens and Archie gets in next to me. I wipe my eyes and sit back and buckle in as Max pulls out of the parking lot.

'Be about half an hour to Malahide,' Max calls out, and I try to hide my smile.

'You're dropping me home? I thought we could have round two tonight.' Archie tries to kiss me on the neck, but I look at him, appalled that he just said that in front of someone.

I nod towards the driver's side and hope he takes the hint to shut up.

Archie stops talking, but he doesn't have his seat belt on and he is trying to make out with me. I let him kiss me, but I'm less than enthusiastic. His hand runs up my leg, and he pulls up the full-length gown so he can touch my knees.

'Archie,' I whisper. 'Stop it.' I throw the bottom of my dress down and I see Max's eye shifting from the rearview mirror to the road.

'Oh, come on, it's not like a driver hasn't seen all sorts.'

He's not even trying to be quiet, and I don't know if he's winding up me, or Max.

'Stop it,' I tell him and push him back into his seat, but he doesn't budge. He's quick when he pins my hand down on the seat and gets his other hand up my dress and between my legs. His lips are on me, and I've turned my head away from him. I've tried to push him off with my free hand and kick away his hand, but I can't.

'Don't be such a prude, you already let me screw you last night.'

57

'Get off me,' I scream. The only other option I'd have would be to head-butt him. Or wait until he's on top of me and try that thing Max showed me where you can use a guy's shirt to pull up and over their head, wrap it around their throat and choke them out.

I don't have to do any of that because I forgot Max was with me. I never felt the car come to a stop on the road or heard his door open.

It's the cold gush of air I feel when the door on the other side of Archie is yanked open and the body that was holding me down, the hand that was roughly trying to coax its way into my dry-as-fuck panties, is gone.

Archie yelps when he realises he's being pulled into mid-air, and he scrambles to find his footing. He might have been fast and strong with me, but he's got nothing on Max.

Before Archie's feet have touched the road, Max has used the move I wanted to and head-butted Archie. The man groans as he falls to the ground and Max picks him up by the shirt collar and drags him off the road, to the sidewalk.

Max slams my door closed and the shivers take me.

Back in the driver's seat, Max tears back into traffic. He doesn't look at me, but all I can do is stare at him. His jaw is clenched, and he's gripping the steering wheel.

After five minutes, we're driving through the tunnel, and I've calmed myself enough that I know I won't burst into tears. I unclip my belt and the beeping tone alerting the hazard dings up front. Max looks into the mirror, but I'm already climbing into the front next to him.

I buckle up and crank up the heating.

Max leans forward and shuffles out of his suit jacket while driving. He hands it over to me and I take it willingly. I wrap it around my gold and sapphire dress, and I know this should be something your date does for you after a night of glamour and fun. Keeps you warm and gets you home safely.

The chill is running right through my bones. I need to heat up. I need to feel like someone will wrap their arms around me and hug me. 'Thank you.' I didn't mean to whisper the words, but apparently, it's all I can manage.

Brona Mills

Rain hits the windshield hard when we get out the north side of the tunnel, onto the M1, and Max flicks the wipers on to full speed. The pelting and monotone sound of the wipers moving back and forth is hypnotic and I focus all my thoughts on the sound and try to figure out how many books could fit in an Amazon truck.

I close my eyes and lay my head on the window. My breathing gets deeper as I run through a meditation app that I've almost memorised perfectly.

Half an hour later, we're pulling into my farming estate house. I let my eyes open, but I don't want to move from here.

The gates open automatically and close tight behind the car.

'Can you make coffee? I'm going to schedule some social media for next week.' There's no way I'm going to just drift off to a pleasant sleep. I'm going to have to exhaust myself first.

'It's ten thirty. Don't you want an early night?'

'Fine, make it tea. And I'll go to bed in a couple of hours.' I open the car door without waiting for Max to do it and search for my keys in my purse.

My hands are shaking and I can't get the key in the lock.

Max is next to me and his hand closes over mine and helps me guide the key in.

'I'm freezing,' I tell him, trying to make excuses for the shaking.

'I know.'

But we both know I'm about to fall apart.

Max locks the door behind us, and I wait in the hallway next to him. It's silly. It's my house, but I feel like I shouldn't move too far away from him. He guides me into the living room with that soft nudge of his hand on my lower back again, and I sit on the couch. Max kneels in front of the fire and gets it lit in less than a minute.

He pulls out some blankets I have for watching movies and wraps them around me. I clasp my hands in his and I sit there without saying anything.

'I'm sorry,' I tell him eventually.

'For what?'

'For putting you in the position that you had to help me.' I backtrack. 'I mean, I know helping me is your job, but this was never what you were supposed to save me from.'

'I didn't deck him for my job, Orchid. You're my friend, and he deserved what he got from me. He actually deserves worse, but that's a dilemma for another day.'

'You knew he was about to turn nasty on me, didn't you? That's why you were looking in the mirror? You never look in the mirror when I'm on a date.'

I wait for an answer, and his eyes look so kind, I want to run my hands over his face and make this the last image I see before I try to sleep tonight.

'Had a feeling, was all.'

'How?'

Max shakes his head, not wanting to answer me.

'I need to know. I mean, I know what happened, but I need to know what the turning point was. The place I should have gotten myself out of the situation before it got that far. If I was ever on my own, I don't want to wait and see what happens.'

'When he kissed you the first time.'

I laugh once. 'That's not much to go on, Max.'

'When you didn't kiss him back, and he was okay with that. That's when you know a guy doesn't care about you. Doesn't mean he's going to attack you, but that should be your warning sign that he's not the one you want to let kiss you.'

I shrug, not really convinced by his thought. 'I'm a bit socially awkward like that on dates. Never really one hundred percent in the headspace with a guy.'

'I'd never be okay with you tolerating me kissing you,' he says fast. 'I'd need you to chase my mouth, just like I'd chase yours.' His voice wavers at the end. 'That's how you'd know if someone really cares, Orchid.'

I stare at him and he stands. 'I'll put the kettle on.'

I want to follow Max into the kitchen to get the tea with him, but I'm still freezing, and I'm slowly heating up here in front of the fire.

Max is back before I have to fret further, and I spit out the words I know I won't say if I wait around any longer.

'Will you stay in the house with me tonight?'

Max hands me the mug, and I wrap both hands around it, my fingers relishing in the boiling water inside the cup.

'I know it's not what we agreed to in the beginning—'

Max cuts me off. 'It's no problem for me to stay. House has been locked up all night, but let me do a quick sweep before we settle in.'

I nod and Max gets to work.

When he returns, I have the TV on and my feet tucked up on the couch, and I drop them to the floor to let him in.

'You want to watch a movie?' I ask.

'Sure.' He toes off his own shoes and rests his feet up on the ottoman. I sit up to share the blanket with him, but he doesn't take any more than I've given him.

I order the new Mike Knight action movie. 'At least it's not a rom-com, right?' I smile.

I'm dreaming.

I can feel the soft haze of floating, and I don't want to leave this imaginary place. The spot right where you have a sense of control over what's happening in your dreams. I'm in bed and there is a delicious man underneath me. The heat of another body and the firmness of his abs under my touch have me searching for more. I've my head resting on his chest and even in my dream state, I know it's Max I'm fantasising about.

He smells like Max. Clean and manly and sharply fresh, like his shower gel.

The feel of his dress shirt under my fingers, playing with the buttons, is something I could get used to. I moan and breathe in his scent. His grip wraps around my waist, holds me tight as he whispers my name, and I push my body into him more.

I move up to get my legs over him and as I crawl, my lips follow up his neck, my mouth opening to inhale him as much as I can, my hands gripping through his hair.

'Orchid!' Max shouts.

Fuck.

61

So not a dream.

I jump up, fully awake, and I've almost mauled Max on the couch.

His hair looks like I've messed it up from some really good dream sex. The morning light shines through the gap in the curtains. I don't even remember the start of the movie, let alone falling asleep.

'Oh my god.' I run my hand over my face, and I can't look at him. I can only look down at the couch, and Max shifts to untangle his legs from me. I'm still sitting on him and try to move to let him up, and I swear, the romance author in me catches sight of his morning wood, and even I know I can't think of a way to make this all okay.

Shit, shit, shit.

This is not good.

This is not a dream or a fantasy or *hot-security guy falls for the woman he is protecting* type story. This is real life and I've just sexually assaulted an employee.

'Please don't sue me,' I say. 'I really didn't mean to do that.' I feel sick.

Max's chest shakes as he tries to hold in his laugh. 'Wasn't planning on suing you. But good to know for future reference.' He winks and lets out a breath. 'I thought you would never wake up.'

'Max,' I slap him on the chest. 'This is serious. I just tried to dream-fuck you.'

Max widens his eyes. 'Well, in that case, it is serious.'

'Oh god, I really shouldn't have said that either.'

Max shakes his head. 'Really shouldn't have.'

There's an awkward pause as Max stands in the living room, and I'm kneeling on the couch.

I run my hand through my hair, and the hair tie falls to the ground. Max picks it up and walks to the kitchen. I follow him out, tripping over my long dress as I scramble off the sofa.

Max puts the coffee pot on and drops my hair tie into a painted jam-jar that one of my nieces made for me when I was home last. I left it on the kitchen windowsill when I returned, and it's now half full with all the other hair ties and pins Max's found around the house.

'Workout in twenty minutes.' Max nods and leaves for his own place.

'Twenty? You normally give me ten minutes' notice. What you got to do so early in the morning it can't wait until we're done?'

Max stops but doesn't turn around. He just shakes his head.

'What?' I call after him as he swings the front door closed. 'I smell that bad in the mornings? You want to shower first?'

My stomach rolls when I remember Archie's touch and smell on me last night. I run through the kitchen and laundry room to the downstairs bathroom. I only crouch over the toilet before I throw up. I wait a second before I bend down and let my knees hit the tiles on the floor and give myself a second before I move. Guess I want a shower before the day starts too.

chapter eight

Orchid

Monday rolls around before I know it. And instead of taking the day off, I keep working to help my assistant, Ailish, organise the London signing next week.

Max's scheduled day off has fallen to mirror my own, and he either hangs around the house with me, or meets his family that he mentioned live in Dublin. A few times he's talked me into hill walking trips around the country.

Now that I think of it, it's not much of a day off for him.

He's always babysitting me.

Ailish is helping me fill and organise and bundle the last of the pre-orders for London.

'You oversold,' I tell her, looking at the stacks of books we've moved into the landing.

'I can't fit this on a plane. I can't even fit this in my car to drive over.'

I stand up and stretch out my back.

Ailish stands next to me. 'You still have the swag bags to bring as well, but if you wait till you get there to pack the bags, it will take up less space to transport them.'

'And by me, you mean us. We're going to have to get there a day early and set this up in the hotel. Just as well we booked adjoining rooms.'

'I'm not coming,' she tells me. 'I cancelled last week. You already know this.'

'Fuck, I knew this, but I forgot to find someone else. I was actually putting it off because I don't know anyone else who would come with me.'

'What about Max?' she asks.

'What about Max?' Max asks from the bottom of the stairs.

I lean over the banister. 'Nothing,' I call down. I shake my head at Ailish. 'I can't ask him to do this,' I whisper.

Max has already climbed the stairs. 'Sure you can. Ask me what?'

'She needs you to be her assistant at the book signing in London. I can't go anymore.'

'Sure,' Max says. 'I'm going to be there, anyway.'

'I thought you could take some of the time off and visit your grandparents?'

'Molly, going to a big event with many people is exactly the time you need me constantly. What's the big deal to come help you haul boxes and hand out a few books?'

I look at Ailish, and she puts her hand on my arm. 'I'll go through everything with him before you guys leave,' she says. 'I'll cancel the flights and book Max's Jeep onto the ferry. We can keep the books boxed, and if we arrange things right, you'll be able to fit everything in that way. I'll keep the adjoining rooms so you can set up, and I'll cancel Max's if that's okay?'

'Okay,' I breathe. 'Thank you both.'

Ailish continues to organise stickers that are shooting out of the printer, while Max gives me a tight smile and goes back down the stairs.

That smile is going to be the death of me.

'So, tell me about the new post approval you put on the readers' group,' I ask Ailish.

Anything work related will help keep my mind off that smile.

'It's easy enough. We have to check the posts every hour. It will be a lot more work upfront, but hopefully it will help to get any nasty comments and posts shut down before they even make it live.'

I shake my head. 'I love my group. It's just a new few people that are creating drama.'

'I know,' she says. 'But drama can fester, and I've been deleting and monitoring loads the past few months. It's just got out of hand. So, I heard from another assistant that this might work. A few weeks of approving posts, and people will learn what they can't post. Then we can go back to normal.'

'Okay.' I nod. 'But you should have told me sooner. If you've been dealing with this on your days off, then I totally owe you big time.'

Ailish nods to me. 'Well, let's just say this mix-up with not coming to the singing makes us even.'

'Deal. And I'll pick you up something nice on the duty-free on the way back!'

She raises her eyebrows. 'I'd much rather get a handbag from Harrod's.'

I laugh. 'Yeah, well, if you had scheduled in an extra day for shopping, that might have been an option.'

'You keep saving me like this, Max, and I'm going to make you come to the American events with me. Next one's Texas. You think we can persuade my dad to get that fancy private jet again?'

Max shrugs. 'Why don't you just have all your online orders shipped straight to your parents' house, then you can get them driven over, and you don't have to bring them on the flight with you.'

'Damn, you're sooo not just a pretty face, are you?'

'I've been told that many times, baby.' He smiles.

The bellboy and Max have both helped me load up two hotel trolleys and we are slowly making the way to the rooms.

Max tips the guy and we keep the trolleys inside the room. The rooms aren't big and the space at the door is taken up. The ferry was less than two hours, but the drive from Holyhead to London has been six hours. I'm wrecked and I don't even comment about the trolley blocking the room door and the fire exit and I let my anxieties simmer below while I try to let my brain catch up with the work I need to do on a frazzled day.

'I'll need the bed and floor space to organise it all.'

Which means I'm going to be sidestepping things in the middle of the night to get to the bathroom. It's going to be tight to work all this out, but at least we have the rest of the day and night to organise ourselves. 'I don't need to be at the venue until two p.m. tomorrow to set up for the pre signings at four.' I'm reassuring myself more than Max. He already has the schedule, and his huge brain probably has it memorised, along with the directions to get there and alternate routes for any roadworks or problems.

Max has opened the adjoining room and comes back to me. 'I left your bag next door. I'll take this one and then you'll have more space to get yourself ready without all these boxes in the way.'

'I can take this room. I'll only keep you awake all night frantically checking I've not forgotten anything.'

Max has already picked up the room phone, and he holds up a menu to me.

I nod and don't care what I eat. I rip some tape off a box and unpack and double-check the orders Ailish printed off for me.

Max joins me, and we organise out the merchandise for the swag bags. I only have enough to cover the first two hundred at my table, but after opening the cases and filling the first ten bags, I realise this is going to take longer than I thought.

A bottle of red wine and two bottles of beer are delivered with the food, and when Max hands me a glass, I take a deep breath of the wine. 'How did you know I need this?'

'Because you need to relax.'

I kick off my shoes and lean against the wall. 'I think this is the first time I've seen you drink alcohol.'

Max takes a swig of the cold beer, and I watch his lips close together as he savours the taste. 'Thought two wouldn't do any damage. I am technically still on the clock.'

'Yes, I guess you are.'

Sucks that I can't just find and keep a friend to hang out with. Apparently, the only two people who get my crazy work schedule and my OCD about how I like things are the people who are paid to be in my life.

I finish the first glass of wine in record time.

'How much does all of this giveaway stuff cost you?'

I roll my eyes. 'Honestly don't ask. I sell a lot of pre-orders for these events, and some more on-the-day sales, but after travel and accommodation, and the swag things, I'm lucky if I break even.' I lean

67

forward and grab the burger off the plate Max has laid on the floor for us. 'But I love this part of the job, and I can afford it. A lot of authors need the book events to top up their income for the year.' I dip my burger and bun into ketchup on the side of the plate and Max makes a grossed-out look.

'Most of the people who'll be there tomorrow are people who are in my readers' group. It's the only chance a lot of them, and me, get to meet each other. The swag is just a way to thank them all for making the trip. They have expenses getting here too, as well as paying for tickets to the event. A lot of people come over from the US and around Europe, so it's nice to let them know I appreciate it.'

'Ailish told me what to expect tomorrow,' Max says. 'And if it's anything like the buzz in your social media groups, it'll be busy.'

'How do you know what's going on in my groups?'

Max shrugs. 'It's my job to check these things out.'

'Oh my god, do you snoop in my readers' group?' I pull up my phone to check if Max is a member. With almost forty thousand people in there, it would be easy to sit in the background and not comment on anything. No one would ever notice that you're there.

Max pulls my phone out of my hand.

'I'm not in there, but my IT guy is. He only flags any unusual activity to the team meetings.'

'You have team meetings about me?' I squeak.

Max looks hurt. 'Of course we do, Orchid. You have twenty-four-hour security on you. What, you think we just cash a cheque and hang out in your living room?'

I lean back and swallow a bite of burger that won't go down as smoothly as it should. I change the subject. I don't want to fight with Max when he's doing a big favour for me. Scratch that. I never want to fight with Max.

'You might get asked to do some line ambassador work, hand out tickets and ask people to come back at certain time intervals. The venue has volunteers for that, but if it gets busy, you might need to help me.'

Max nods.

'And keep the swag bags next to my table topped up. The pickup orders are alphabetically organised, and we'll label up the boxes tonight. So if someone in line has a pre-order, they'll give you their printed code and you can give them their books. There's a collection document on the iPad they need to sign and you just hit save. Anything else is cash only.'

'Got it. Ailish already showed me how it works. And I'm on lunch and coffee duty, although I'll probably pay a volunteer to get those things for us. As your security guy, I won't be comfortable going too far away from you to run errands.'

'Fair enough. Some people might ask if you're the model for the next cover.' I bite my lip and hope he doesn't ask why.

'Why?'

Oh lordy.

'Orchid?' Max's no-nonsense, serious tone should make me shudder with fear, but that's never the type of shudders he gives me.

'Well, some authors bring the cover models along for photo ops and signings, too. The models love it as it boosts their social media followings and helps them get future shoots. You might even see some photographers there too who specialise in novel graphics.'

'Why would anyone think I was your next model?'

I tilt my head. 'You're hot, Max, you know fine well you are. And you're toned and you have a brilliant smile when you talk to people, so it's going to be the first thing they think. I mean, why else would you be there?'

'Hm.' He shrugs and takes a bite of his burger. 'I thought it might have to do with the fact that you told your reader group that your new driver was a *hot-as-fuck cover model who you might sneak a picture of and save the photographer's fee for the next cover.'*

I gasp and throw fries at Max. 'You *are* in my group, you sneaky little fucker.'

Max laughs as he dodges the fries and holds up his hands. 'In my defence, this is your own fault. It was flagged, and I had to go in and have a look. Then I just stayed there in case you carried out your threat.'

I shake my head. 'Why do you always make me say things you already know?'

69

'I can't get in any pictures, Orchid.'

'Oh no, I know that. I was never serious. It was a while ago and just a joke, to make light of the fact you were moving into my house.'

'I mean tomorrow. I can't be in the background of any pictures, so we need to set up your banners for photos and ask people to only take pictures there. I've already spoken to venue security. We can get them to run interference around your line, and I have a list of all the scheduled photographers on the day. The venue is being very accommodating.'

My heart drops. 'Please don't tell me you caused a scene, Max. This is the best part of my job. I'd hate for people to think I was a diva.'

Max shakes his head. 'I know that. Both the venue and the organisers were more than happy with an inconvenience fee. I'm a smooth talker when I want to be, Orchid.'

Don't I know it.

He mistakes my silence for scepticism.

'You don't think so?'

Max slides the plate of food between us to the side and sits up on his knees. Leaning forward, closing in the small space between us, he says, 'I might not be as imposing as your First Responder's Brothers series.'

I hold my breath as he closes the distance and breathes right in my face. I don't know what's more shocking: the fact that he's going to kiss me or that he knows about my books. Shut up, Orchid, and live in the real-life swooning moment.

'But I can deliver on a promise.'

My gaze drops to Max's lips and my tongue darts out, wetting my lips and rehydrating my dry mouth. It's hot in here.

Max watches my lips, and the serious seduction face he had on takes on a look of regret.

Shit.

He pulls back and jumps to his feet. 'Told you I got the smooth talking down.' He's trying to keep his voice light, like our usual banter, but there's a forced feeling, like he must feel like shit for almost kissing me, and I almost let him.

'You know what else we need?' Max sidesteps the merchandise on the floor and makes it to the phone and asks for the concierge. 'Can we have a pack of climbing hooks? Large ones, twenty at least.' He pauses. 'No later than midnight, please.'

Max hangs up the phone. 'You need to be in bed before midnight.' He nods. 'We can hook the swag bags through them and that way it's easier to carry in without them falling or tipping over. We can even hook them through the coat hangers for the trolley.' He points at the small wardrobe near the door.

'That's a great idea.' I clap my hands, remembering that there's no real swoon and comfortableness to be sought after by some hot guy who works for you. Not in RL anyway. 'A plan is coming together.'

Max grimaces. 'Yeah, but now you've got to hope the concierge doesn't think we want them for any weird sex tricks.'

I look at his mouth, that's just uttered a flirt. I really should distract myself from these thoughts about Max. I thump my head back on the wall, harder than I intended. 'Great.' I pretend to be offended that someone might think Max is going to tie me up for *weird sex tricks*, but the sarcasm comes out weaker than I'm happy with. I'd love nothing more than Max to show me what *a freak in the sheets* is like.

'Payback's a bitch, Molly Murphy.' Max winks and I love the fact he's used my book name.

The hotel is hosting the signing downstairs in its largest conference room, so we don't have to travel in the morning.

Max is leading the way through the lobby and has got a member of the hotel security and a bellboy to help with the trolley. It doesn't take long for the setup with the extra hand, even though Max spends a lot of time on his phone. He must do official work, as he has his serious face on.

The room is as quiet as it will be for the day, even though there is a constant background noise of people moving tables and pulling out roller banners for their setups. We only have another few minutes before the doors open, and the wave of people descends

71

upon us. I'm lucky my readers have central places to come visit me. My line always fills up fast, and sometimes security have to hand out ticket numbers for people to come back in the afternoon, which means I have to find a nice balance of taking the time to sign the books and post for photos and a minute of chat, but keep the line moving efficiently so I can meet everyone who showed and lined up.

It's a half hour before my scheduled lunch break when Max stops the line and comes to speak to me quietly at the table.

'Orchid, we have to go.'

'Go where?' I ask him.

'There was a threat made this morning, and this is too public a place for you to be.'

I roll my eyes and lean back in my chair, deflated. 'LA is a long way away, Max. No one is going to bother coming to a book signing to the one member of the Rock family who isn't even famous. And call me Molly,' I hiss. 'This is the one place I never want outed for being part of a reality family.'

Max darts his eyes to me. 'Who knows that?'

'Knows what?' I ask.

'The threat was made on social media about outing the family for who they really are. So who knows that you don't want to be outed as a member of the Rock family?'

I throw my hands up. 'I don't know. Everyone in LA who knows who I am there?'

'Time to go.'

'No,' I hiss. 'This is my life, and I won't let some person connected to my family's career affect mine. Today is a big day for me. Every person behind you in that line has bought tickets to come here and has lined up for hours. And you're putting me off schedule.'

I look around the side of him and nod to the person at the start of the line to make their way over.

Max moves out of the way and lets them pass.

'And, Max, can you bring my lunch to the table?' I ask. 'I'm not taking a break. I'll eat here.' I smile, a little bitchy, dismissing him back to work.

Max checks his phone and I swear it only takes seconds for four other security guys, dressed in plain clothes, to appear at my line.

I hadn't been looking for them, but now that they are flanking my table and taking up sentry duty, it's ridiculous how they thought they would blend into the crowd as romance readers.

The bellboy from this morning appears with my coffee and sandwich and places it on the table.

Great. Now I look like a diva with an entourage. I look at Max and I'm not sure who or what has me annoyed at the ridiculousness of my new staffing. There is a small shriek coming from the line in front of me, followed by someone shouting. When I look up, Max has already moved in front of me. Facing the line, he moves towards people who are arguing. When he steps forward, someone is pushed farther up the line and they fall onto my table. I get up and try to reach out to catch the girl who is stumbling, but between us both, the table moves and collapses, and my hot coffee that's just arrived spills all over my arm. I gasp at the heat sensation as it passes over my arm, but I know it's not serious. Max grabs me off the floor, while everyone in the line moves forward to help rescue the table and its contents and the other girl who fell.

I can't even try to help her up, as Max is pulling me by my good arm towards the back of the room and walking swiftly with me through the fire escape and down the stairs.

'It was an accident,' I yell as I pull my arm free from Max's grasp. 'I can't run off over some spilled coffee.' I look down at the soaking sleeve of my shirt and wince. When I pull the sodden material away, there is an angry red stain covering the inside of my forearm. 'Shit,' I say.

'Let's get some ice on that.' Max nods to the bottom door where we're met by hotel security and led towards the kitchens.

I'm not there when my promo materials are packed up and brought back up to the room. After talking to security and reviewing the camera recordings, Max was satisfied that it was indeed an accident. But by the time my arm was cooled and Max's security instincts tepid, the signing day was over and I wouldn't be able to go back even if I wanted to.

73

Two security guys stay outside the room, while Max brings everything inside.

'I cancelled your dinner tonight,' Max tells me.

I collapse onto the bed. I'm a mixture of exhausted from the drama of today and deflated that I won't get to mix with my author network. I like to hang out with them on the rare occasion our schedules have us attending the same events.

Part of me is glad I get to curl up in bed and chill for the night, so I let it go.

'I told you not to interfere with my work.' I look up at him from the bed.

Max nods. 'I know. But if there is a threat, your safety trumps everything. Even your job.'

I sit in silence, and Max moves for the adjoining door to his room. 'If you need me, just call out, okay?'

I nod and he hands me the panic button alarm he gave me on the first day in Dublin. 'You forgot to pack this,' he says.

I softly take it out of his hand and slip it into my phone case. 'Won't happen again.' I narrow my eyes at him.

When he closes the door, I pull out my laptop and let my fingers tap on the keys until I find a rhythm. Before I know it, I'm writing a death scene of my main character and crying my eyes out. I never kill off my characters, but I guess right now I need something tangible to grieve.

chapter nine

Orchid

On the ride back home, my ears are still ringing. I can hear the blood pumping through my ears, and I'm not sure if it's the exhaustion of a packed weekend, coming down off the adrenaline high that's been building for weeks, or the travel on a rough sailing.

But it's all background noise to be here with Max. Despite the argument yesterday, he gives me a sense of Zen in the chaos. The usual bone vibrations and dizziness of trying to keep all my thoughts in order aren't there.

If Ailish had been with me, I'd be driving and concentrating and talking about scheduling future signings.

Max lets me play audition pieces through the Bluetooth speaker for new narrators for my next audio book release. So technically I am still getting through work decisions, but Max's humour at making fun of the narrators makes it feel like fun. Exactly how this job used to be in the beginning, and not how it's progressed into the worry of every decision possibly breaking my career into a pile of crumbs.

'I like this one,' Max says when I play Irish narrator, Jason Diamond. 'You can understand him better than the others, and he sounds like that First Responder feel you go for.'

I side-eye Max from the passenger seat. 'It unnerves me that you know so much about my new series. How long did you spend creeping on my group page?'

75

War and books

Max smiles and shakes his head. 'I may have read some of your books. You can tell a lot about a person from what they read. So I figured the same must be true about what an author writes?'

We're on the motorway, almost home, driving well under the 120 speed limit, when Max's phone rings in the cup holder between us.

I cut off the radio and the narrator, while Max frowns at the name on the phone. He answers and puts the phone to his ear.

'You're not supposed to do that,' I hiss at him, trying to disconnect my phone from the Bluetooth and allow him to run his phone through the radio.

Max listens to the call while I hiss at him.

'Max, put the call on speaker and I'll hold the phone for you at least.'

Max's ignoring me. How anyone can't be distracted by someone talking to them while they are also on the phone is beyond me.

'Understood.' Max hangs up the call and clears his throat. 'There was some vandalism at your house earlier.'

'What?' I twist in my seat to look at Max.

'Your housekeeper reported it to the security company this morning when she showed up.'

I twist my watch around my hand. 'It's almost four. Why didn't they ring us beforehand?'

'They did.' Max keeps his eyes on the road. 'We'd already checked out of the hotel when I got the call, so it was agreed to keep on route.'

'Agreed? By whom?'

'By your team, Orchid. We have contingencies and strategies based on threat levels. By the time I got the first call, it was already established that the vandalism was to the outside of the property only. The Gardai have been around. The security firm is on location. It's clear for us to return. The security team just finished their sweep for anything left behind, so I decided not to inform you of anything until I had to.'

'Did anyone break in?'

'Doesn't appear so. Security feeds have been checked from all cameras, and the house was still secure when the Gardai escorted your housekeeper inside. Everything looks to be in order.'

I slump in my seat and Max veers to the left to take the exit off the motorway, and traffic on the outskirts of town slows us down.

My mind can't stop ticking over, my stomach rolls, and I wish I had some Rescue Remedy handy instead of packed away in the trunk. What if someone had got inside, and my office had been destroyed? All my documents and files are backed up, but it would take me days to put things back together. And there are things that aren't replaceable. Things that aren't savable. Like some handwritten notes scrawled on scraps of paper, ideas that came to me while I've been doing something else, and I've written it down before it's fallen out of my head. Or charts and drawings of imaginary buildings and home layouts I've come up with and use for reference. Pictures and trinkets that readers have sent me.

Then the question hits me. 'What the hell do you mean, *left behind*?'

'You really want to know?'

'Yes,' I hiss as Max pulls off the carriageway, onto the back roads.

'The worst-case scenario is traps and bombs being planted.'

'Bombs?' My eyes widen. Not that I think that might be left behind for me. But I kind of forget that Max was a soldier. That he's dealt with real-life war and fighting. I mean, I knew he was a soldier, but from what I've seen around my house, he's just Max. A highly organised and good at his job, personal security guy who keeps my parents from worrying about me.

'That was the worst-case scenario, in high-end business sabotage cases. For this type of case, the celebrity angle, I would be more concerned about cameras and recording devices being installed in your house or your computer. We have investigative protocols for this, and we've been given the all clear, so don't worry about something that hasn't happened.'

77

'Easy for you to say. It might not be a break-in this time, but it has been in my parents' house in the past. I know it's not the kind of job you're used to, but this is a big deal in my world. To think that someone has been snooping around my home? It might *be* a break-in at my place next time.'

I feel the tears welling in the back of my eyes. I take three deep breaths to get myself under control. I shouldn't be emotional, but it's years of built-up frustration knowing that my family's crazy careers and chasing their dwindling fame and fortune have finally broken into my life.

Something I've consciously placed physical and emotional distance from for years. I could have easily been included in the original series of the show. I could have had cameras follow me around in a docu-type series. I could have signed a contract and collected a salary and cashed in endorsements, just like my sisters and brothers did.

But I chose peace and personal privacy instead.

'You're not letting your family's lives bleed over yours, Orchid. But you've left yourself vulnerable too. Now that there is proper security on the whole family, there should be fewer incidents.' Max turns to me. 'Don't let anything that's happened to them control your life, Orchid.'

'I'm not.'

Max looks back at the road. 'You're scratching your fingers. You're tapping your foot. You only do that when you get really anxious.'

I look down at my hands and drop them on my thigh so I don't start fidgeting again. I consciously stop my feet from tapping.

The gates to the house open automatically with the sensor on Max's car and we slow down on the approach to the turn. There's a security truck outside my gate and when the gates open, a second vehicle sitting on the driveway.

'This seems a little excessive for some spray paint on the gates,' I say. But when I see the words sprayed in red, I stop myself from arguing.

Stop hiding

'What the fuck does that mean? 'Who the hell wrote that?' I shout at Max.

Why would someone try to scare me like this?

I fidget with my hands over the seat belt for something to do. Not sure whether to stay put or flee out of the car.

'Wait in the car until I open your door.' Max gets out his side and is at my door quicker than I could have thought.

'They'll be here for a couple of days.' Max nods to the security van in the driveway. 'Until we're confident this wasn't connected to what's been happening with your family.'

I grab Max's arm before he gets to my front door. 'Tell me what you know. Don't blindside me going in there.'

'All doors and windows were still locked and the cameras don't show anyone making it onto the property, and nothing near the house. No vehicles were seen on the cameras, just someone ran up to the gate. No face can be seen. Nothing was out of place inside the house. Nothing looks to be stolen, but we'll need you to confirm. They left something inside the mailbox. Camera's seen them place it inside. The Gardai took it as evidence.'

'What was it?'

'An Orchid.'

chapter ten

Orchid

Max follows me around the house as I inspect each room and confirm to myself that no one has been inside.

When Max's phone rings, he indicates he wants me to listen in and we sit in the living room while he activates his speaker.

James, one of Max's security team in the UK, lets us know everything is quiet with my family in LA, and after speaking to the Gardai in Dublin this morning, the team thinks that the focus of the threats has more to do with me than my family.

'That's absurd. I'm not even known in LA,' I tell them.

Over the speaker, James answers me, 'It makes more sense for the threats to be from a personal interaction. Either someone you know or used to know. Or even met or dated briefly. I think keeping the focus on the family, and you as a secondary target, is wrong. We need to assume that you are a direct target and maybe even the primary concern.'

I stand up when I talk. 'Some spray paint isn't something to get mad over,' I say.

'No, but we were warned of a threat in your social media,' Max tells me. 'I thought it was going to be while we were in London, but it was here at your home instead. We have to assume that they are connected to your family's threats.'

'People are always writing crazy things on social media. You can't take everything seriously or even read it all. That's why I have Ailish edit and delete anything with negativity in it. Otherwise the place could get overrun with nasty stuff.'

'Who deletes what?' James asks.

'Ailish, my assistant. She monitors my socials and gets rid of anything that's particular nasty.'

Max leans back in his chair. 'We need to speak to her and see what and how much she's deleting. There may have been more indicators or evidence that we're not even seeing.'

I shake my head. 'It's not evidence. It's the internet. Today, for example, she spent hours calming down the bad vibes about me not coming back after my table collapsed. There are a couple of people being really nasty about it. That's it. I don't have a stalker. This is nothing to do with me,' I argue.

'They know your name.'

'Leaving a flower behind in someone's mailbox doesn't have to be creepy.' I shake my head at Max, knowing that it's as creepy as hell. Especially when it's a flower of my name.

'Someone's mad you're hiding as Molly Murphy when you're really someone else,' Max says.

'We need to up the personnel out there with you guys,' James says.

My eyes widen at Max. 'I don't need a bunch of guys at my house,' I hiss.

Max holds his hand up to me and speaks to James. 'I can ring an army buddy I have in the UK. If he's available, it's only an hour's flight, so that will be the quickest option. Let me get back to you.' Max hangs up the phone and turns to me. 'You won't even know he's here. I'll keep our schedule and work the same, and Cameron is backup only.'

He nods at me, and I mirror his action, agreeing to another intrusion in my life.

The spray paint has been stripped from the gate, but the wood will need to be treated and painted in the morning. Groceries have been delivered earlier when Ailish was here. It's Monday after all.

'So, let's get cooking.' I try to sound upbeat. 'I'm starving.'
Max looks worried.
'What now?'

81

'Your cooking might be more dangerous than what happened here today.'

I take a threatening step towards him, taunting him to speak again.

'Zip it.' I brush my fingers over his lips, imitating a twisting movement, like I used to do with my sister when she pissed me off. But instead of swatting my hand away like I would expect, Max holds his breath.

'Wine,' I shout and spin at the top of the stairs, away from Max. 'Let's get drinking, and you can cook since you're such a critic.'

In the kitchen, I open a bottle of cab sav since it's the only wine Max would consider drinking and jump up onto the counter. Max looks in the fridge and hums.

'You want chicken or steak?'

'Either,' I say. 'Keep it light, though.' I have a tub of moulding putty that I stole from my niece a year ago and open it up and start stretching and rolling it between my hands. The feeling between my fingers has helped keep me distracted from lots of things over the years. I kneed the putty in the counter and stretch it out over my knuckles. The cool, smooth texture and the strength I need to put into my fingers helps me ring out tension I'd otherwise be clenching through my spine.

Max pulls out some veggies and salad bags and nods at the cupboard between my legs. 'Gonna need in there.'

Normally I would expect some sort of smirk or humour from him, but his neck is red, and please god, I hope he just blushed.

The wine has got to me. It must have. Why else would I open my legs and stare him out. I'm never this brave. I never flirt. Hell, I don't know how to flirt. Is it flirting or downright nasty harassment from someone you work for?

Max takes the bait and obviously is much cooler in this situation than I am. He struts over to me and the door he wants into and nudges my knees farther apart. Looking me in the eye, he says, 'You really want to play this game?'

Before I have a chance to be seductive and wrap my legs around his back and pull him in for a Goodreads-award-worthy kiss, just like I would write for one of my couples, Max jerks my legs forward and catches me. My ass slips off the edge of the marble.

I gasp at the disappointment in where I know this is going.

He swings me around and within a second places me on the floor in front of the counter.

'You get all sorts of brave when you're drinking, Orchid. Just don't do that shit when you're sober, or I might see if you're for real.'

He tosses a capsicum at me and I scramble to catch it, while he opens the damn cupboard and gets out the glass mixing bowl.

'You're on salad duty.'

I snatch the bowl out of his hand. 'Oh, really.' I mock laugh, waiting for some witty comment to enter my brain, but I've got nothing, and I'm left hanging.

The rest of dinner prep is in silence. It's the normal comfortable come-down after a rough day, and I love the breathing time to process the day's events.

'You should call your parents,' Max tells me when we take our plates to the table.

I swallow a gulp of wine down and wait for it to settle. 'Okay.' I nod.

'Seriously. I've watched you dodge their calls since I got here. You always call back when you know you'll get their voicemail.'

Shit. 'No, I don't.'

'Yes, you do. It's so obvious. And you never pick up when they return the call.'

'I'm busy,' I tell him.

'And that's what you tell them. But guess what, your family, who works sixty-plus hours a week, still manage the time to chase your calls around. They want to be a part of your life, but you avoid them.'

'I avoid their drama.' I point my fork full of chicken in the air.

'They know you're lying to them, and you still think it's them who are the bad guy. Maybe you're to blame for the distance in the relationship that bugs you so much.'

'Lying about what?'

'Thanksgiving, for one. You told them you couldn't take the time off, but you've already booked two days off in your schedule to meet the American Overseas group in Dublin for Thanksgiving celebrations.'

'It's just easier not to have to travel.'

'Why, you not happy that daddy won't send the company jet to pick you up this time?'

Max has some stubble growth from yesterday and today that's grown longer than he usually leaves it, and I'd really like to reach out and run my hands over it. See what it feels like. It might even feel better than putty in my hands. To have a pretty face for my fingers to explore would certainly be a distraction.

'For your information, I have no problem travelling commercial.'

Max laughs, a full-blown laugh. 'Orchid, do you have any idea how spoiled that whole sentence sounds?'

'What do you want from me, Max?'

'Go home for the holidays. Try to repair some of the damage you feel is in your life. And maybe you'll not get as much resistance from your family as you think there is.'

I chew on my food and push some of the baby kale leaves around the plate. 'Do *you* want to go home for Thanksgiving?' I completely forgot that Max might like some time off. That he might want to see his family. That he's here for work, and not just living with me like a roommate who I never get sick of hanging around.

Max shrugs. 'Sure I do. But this isn't a decision to make for me. I've worked plenty of holidays. This one can be the same.'

'Okay, I'll go. With the extra security hanging around soon, I might as well be in the chaos of LA. Might be a good idea to give you some time off, right? Don't want you burning out, do we?'

'Orchid—'

'It's fine, Max. This is a good reason to push me home. I'll be tucked up at my parents' house, so you can have the time with your folks. I know you call them every day. I hear you in the other room, you know.'

Max nods. 'As long as you won't be miserable. I know how much your keyboard suffers when you're trying to write pissed off.'

I nudge Max with my elbow and abandon the food for some more wine.

'You okay there?'

'Would it be weird if I asked you to move into the house with me?'

'Not at all.' Max looks at his food and concentrates on eating.

'If it's weird, it's okay. It's just that, well. I didn't want you in my house when I didn't know you, but I know you now. Hell, I trust you more than I trust any man I've ever dated. And after today'—I swallow down the lump of accepting that maybe I need someone in my life to look after me if there is a stalker out there—'I'd feel safer with you here if anything ever happened again.'

Max looks at me this time. 'That's a good idea, Orchid. And I'll liaise with your family's security team and get a structure in place for you over the holidays. You'll need to stay in their main house.'

I nod. 'Already thought that.'

'How long do you want to go for?'

'I don't know. Four, five days? Could go a week if you want more time with your parents? If my keyboard complains, we can cut the trip short, tell everyone I have a book related emergency.' I chuckle.

'Whatever you decide, I'll work around.' He looks at me and grins. 'You think there's any chance Daddy dearest can call in some favours and wangle the jet again to come pick us up?'

I spurt out a laugh and have to put my wineglass down. 'Now who's spoiled, Maxy boy?'

'Hey, tell him we'll split the fuel and airport charges and staff billing. All it will cost him is a favour to his boss.'

'Go halves?' I raise my eyebrows at him. 'Do you even have any idea how much a transatlantic flight costs?'

Max shrugs. 'I can file it as a business expense. Totally tax deductible.'

'No, it's too much. Hell, I wouldn't even bring myself to spend that kind of money on a plane. Here's the deal.' I pick up the wineglass. 'I'll ask Daddy dearest to pay, and I'll tell him we're home

85

for a week. That I need to bring my work.' I throw my hand around my office. 'Some books or whatever, and it will be easier to have the jet for that length of stay. If he says no, then'—I put my hand over my heart—'I will spring for first-class tickets for us.'

'First class, damn, you're really going all out,' Max mocks. 'Was there ever a scenario that I was expected to travel in business?'

When I laugh, I accidentally snort into my wineglass. 'Well, you've come a long way up on this job. The day I met you, I was going to send you packing on economy.'

'Ouch.'

Max clears the plates and I load the dishwasher.

'I'm going to pack my bag and do a perimeter check. Lock the front door until I come back, okay?'

My heart rate picks up. 'I'll make sure the guest bed down here is made up. We can move everything else over tomorrow for you.'

I grab Max's hand on the way out, meaning to get his attention and convey the seriousness when I give him my appreciation. But the look he gives me, then our tangled hands, sends heat over my skin and makes me nervous to speak.

'Thanks,' I whisper and drop my gaze. Damn, girl. That was a shit appreciation.

Max nods and pulls his hand out of mine on his way out of the kitchen.

It only takes me a minute to pull out the sheets and make the downstairs bed. Everything is in order in the wardrobe there, just in case I ever had someone stay over.

I don't undress. I don't even bother to check the windows are all closed. Something I used to do twice before bed. Max will take care of it.

But I have to stop obsessing over him.

I pull the duvet up and tuck myself into the fluffy heat and feel my body sink into the sheets. I need to get over him.

The library or online, right? The only two places I'm ever going to meet someone.

I take my phone off the cabinet and open up Tinder.

I'm swiping for half an hour when Max appears on my screen as a match.

I don't touch anything, even though I want to screenshot the picture and keep it on my phone. Or at least zoom in and see his face up close. But shit, what if I accidentally swipe the wrong way? His picture is gorgeous. He looks so happy when he's relaxed. The LA sun shines in the background, highlighting his face, his smile. Good Christ, how the hell am I not going to think about him all night now?

I close the app on my phone and put my hand over my mouth to stop the wine giggles from escaping. That's a fast online meet-up, by any standards.

Moving to text messages, I pull up Max's name and type out a message.

I'm not hiding away
If all the crazies are online, then the library wins.
Lunchtime, tomorrow.

chapter eleven

Orchid

I've been at the library every afternoon for a full week, and the only people who are here during the working day are retired or mums with their toddlers.

This plan is sucking more every day I show up. Two hours with my laptop at a table, pretending to research and browse the aisles. Even Max is fed up, and he's taken to grabbing the first seat he can find when he walks in the door. Cameron, a Scottish ex-soldier, flew in from the UK and is now the new resident of my cottage. Max was right. Cameron stays out of the way and I hardly notice he's there.

And there have been no more incidents online, or at my house, or in LA—which means either nothing was connected at all, or the extra security has done the trick. Either way, I'm over it. My work is already suffering from the background stress I'm trying to pretend isn't there.

Productiveness wise, the library isn't bad. The change of scenery has been good, but I miss my slippers and coffee on demand from my kitchen.

My trip to the bathroom has the security guard smile at me. 'Third time this week you've been here. You must study hard.'

Damn. Security guard is the only male here under the age of sixty. Heck, he's under the age of thirty. How did I not spot this earlier? And he's cute. And has a job, and talks to everyone who passes. Overall, a nice guy. Huh.

I put my hand out to introduce myself. 'I'm Or—Molly.' Damn, that's the first time I've ever slipped up.

I'll need to tell Max to stop calling me by my name. I've gotten so used to it again.

'Scott.' He smiles again.

'I'm not a student. I'm just here for the books and the space to work.'

'Grand. So,' he says. 'Where're you from? That accent doesn't belong around here.'

'I'm from Los Angeles, but I've lived here for a while.'

'Oh, a Yank. How very exotic.'

'Well, that's what I thought about the Irish. It's why I moved here.'

'And why did you stay?' he jokes.

I laugh a little too loud and Max turns in his seat near the door to look at me.

Now or never. I've never asked a guy out to his face. Online is easy. You can take the rejection and delete the guy. But in front of your face is brutal.

God, just do it, Orchid, there's been too long a silence now.

'If you want anyone to show you around,' he says. 'I can meet you one night for drinks.'

Huh, didn't even need to pluck up the courage.

'Actually, when I say I've been here a while, I mean, I've been here almost ten years. Know my way around by now.'

Scott nods and tries to hold his smile.

Damn, I wasn't rejecting him.

'But it would be nice to go out. Lunch maybe, or coffee, if you're free one day.'

Scott smiles again. 'Sure. We close here at six. You normally stay till then, don't you?'

Today, right now? With Max waiting around? Fuck.

'Okay.' Swallow that fear and put yourself out there.

'I need to lock up once we close. But how about I meet you in the hotel next door, six-fifteen? We can grab some food and drinks there.'

'Great.'

Now, how the hell am I going to be able to pee in the room right behind his desk, when I've just made a date with him?

Can't go back to the library. That will look like I forgot to pee. I take a deep breath and keep walking to the bathroom.

It's a dirty feeling in here. Blue lighting to stop the druggies injecting, which means the cleaners can't see properly to clean the place. Everything must be dirty.

I hover over the toilet and try not to touch much. It's the only thing I hate about this place, and I'm in love with libraries as a core value.

I try to wash my hands with minimum contact with the faucets. I really hope Scott has a better bathroom to wash his hands in every day. God, ew. I'm going to go on a drink and/or dinner date with someone who may or may not have good hand-washing facilities at work.

This doesn't feel okay.

I unlock the door and pull it open, using tissue paper over my hands, swing the heavy door open, and drop the paper in the trash on my way out. Scott isn't at his station on my way back.

Neither is Max. I look for him when I get fully inside the main library room and see him standing near my table at the back of the room, staring out the window at the street outside.

He turns when I get closer.

'Thought I better watch your computer since you were taking so long.'

'Thanks, but it's not like I had the shits,' I joke.

'God forbid in those bathrooms. Got yourself a date, I heard.'

I roll my eyes and pull out my chair. 'Do you listen to all my conversations?' I whisper.

'Only the good ones. Mostly you're boring, so that little forced giggle was the highlight of my day.' Max winks and instead of returning to his seat at the front of the room, he grabs a book off the shelf and takes a seat next to me.

I stare at him. He's never taken a seat next to me here. He's always maintained his 'working' persona. Hell, he's never interrupted me while I'm working before.

'You don't mind, do you?'

'What's with the pissed off tone?' I ask.

'No tone here.'

I sigh and stretch out my back when I see Scott walking from the computer section, through the stacks toward the front door.

He sees me at the table but doesn't smile back at me.

When I turn around, Max is staring him out.

'Do you mind?' I slap Max's book closed.

It falls out of his hand and clatters on the table. Wasn't like he was really reading it.

'What?' he says. 'Guy can't handle a bit of competition or pressure from the security team, then he's not worth the bother.'

'Oh really? You were the one who told me to date people I meet offline. Well, there you go.' I wave my hand out.

'Shh.' Max smirks. 'This is a library.' He picks up the book and turns to page one.

I look at the bright cover on the alien-romance book he pulled off the shelf.

'Do you even know who Elizabeth Stephens is?'

'Not a clue.' Max keeps reading the young adult book and doesn't look at me again for the two more hours it takes for the place to close.

chapter twelve

Orchid

It's six forty and I'm sitting alone in the Bracken Court Hotel lounge and I'm trying not to drink too fast. The glass in front of me is nearly empty and I'm about to order another when I realise the approaching 7:00 p.m. means he's not coming.

Thank god for phones. I can at least sit here and pretend I've been busy and haven't been waiting for someone.

I open up my readers' group, and am about to tell them I've been stood up and need an exit strategy when I catch sight of a guy coming towards me from the bar.

It's not Scott, but some guy in a cheap suit, carrying a glass of red and a cheesy grin. Like he's the cat that's got the cream. Like he thinks he's a knight in fucking armour and is going to save me from the despair of being stood up. Well, he doesn't realise that blondes aren't my type. Neither are the creepers who think it's okay to bring a drink to a girl themselves. It might be laced with Rohypnol or some other shit. Doesn't he know that's the reason you send the barman with the drink? Or at least wait until she's agreed that you *can* buy her a drink?

Heck, even give the girl money so she can go buy her own— actually, that's pretty funny. I'll need to write that one down.

He smiles at me. Christ, he thought I was smiling at him, not laughing at my own stupid joke.

When he's close enough that there's no mistake he's on his way to my table and not somewhere else, I open my mouth to tell him I'm just leaving when someone sits at my table.

'Sorry I'm late, babe.' Max pulls his chair in and turns to the guy. 'Oh good, you ordered drinks. I'll have a coffee, please.'

The guy who was about to interrupt me looks annoyed when his jaw slacks in horror at the mistake. 'I don't work here,' he scoffs.

Max looks him up and down. He's giving him the stern *don't fuck with me* look. Max makes a show of looking around us. We're the only table this far back and against the wall, so there's nowhere else the guy was bringing the drink to.

'Then what you doing with the wine, dude?' Max asks.

The guy realises that he's just got shot down, and not even by me. By my date. My fake date.

Realising that he won't be delivering the drink, he mutters an apology and retreats to the bar.

Max sighs as he leans back in his chair, and when he sees me staring at him, he shuts his mouth. He's waiting to assess my mood. He doesn't argue often with me. He normally waits until I argue myself out of my own point, which is annoying, really. God, I should really focus on his faults more often.

Sometimes smugly annoying. Check.

That's it. Maybe I'll find more, now that I'm actively keeping watch and noting them.

Neither Max nor I speak. We just stare at each other over the table. What the fuck is he thinking?

My heart picks up speed, and I have to take a deep breath.

Max smiles and leans in. 'So this one time I was sixteen and got stood up—'

I roll my eyes. 'Oh god, this is not going to make me feel any better,' I tell him.

'What?' He shrugs. 'It's a good embarrassing story, and I'm trying to save you from the same fate.'

'You got stood up once in your whole life, when you were sixteen. I'm twenty-eight. Believe me, my embarrassment is worse.'

'Really?' Max leans back. ''Cause I don't see this night ending with you getting your clothes stolen.'

'Okay, I was not expecting that. Explain.'

93

War and books

Max calls the waitress over and we order two coffees and dinner. While we're waiting, he reveals some horror stories of his youth and I have the most relaxed dinner date I've ever had.

Dessert and tea are ordered and I cover my mouth and laugh. 'I've talked your ear off this whole time and I haven't even asked you anything. Are you looking forward to seeing your family? It's been almost two months since you saw them, right?'

'My parents came for a visit about three weeks ago, and it's not like technology isn't great for keeping in touch.'

My mouth drops. 'Your parents were here, and you never told me? OMG, Max, you should have taken time off—how long did you even get to see them?'

'It was a flying visit. They were en route to London to visit my grandparents. I had enough time.' He waves off my embarrassment. 'Once you lock yourself in your writing cave, I get more time off than you realise. It was when you were editing the first draft of *Hidden Alive.*'

She squints her eyes at me. 'That book isn't released yet. How do you know the title?'

Max shrugs. 'It's all over your social media groups.'

'As long as you're not hacking my browser history.' I chuckle nervously. 'You know an author's search history is completely for research. Whatever you may or may not find on there is completely legitimate, right?'

'Of course.' He raises his eyebrows at me and I toss a beer mat at him.

'Stop teasing and tell me about your family. I know nothing and I feel bad since you've been living in my house.'

'Not much to tell. You see my work, you hear me on the phone with the other boys.'

'Your partners, right? You met them in the army. Why did you choose to go into service?'

Max sighs. 'Oh, that's a life story that needs something a lot stronger than coffee.'

'Tell me.' My tone softens more than I realised, and I stare into Max's eyes.

'When I was three, my biological father showed up and caused a lot of problems for my mom. She was single, and she panicked. I remember my grandma taking me into my room to distract me as my mom packed bags and was getting ready for us to run.'

I swallow the lump in my throat. 'Oh god, Max, that's awful.'

He waves his hand up to dismiss my empathy, but instead of switching the subject, he keeps talking.

'We were lucky. My mom had two very good friends who helped her out. One of whom, she later married and became my dad. He's the only man who's ever earned that title from me. Even after they divorced, he still stayed in my life, like a father should. He and my mom functioned together mostly and co-parented me. And three years ago, they sorted out whatever shit drove them apart, and they got married again.'

'Wow, that's a good story.'

Max nods. 'Point is, despite being so young, I remembered the panic she had when she thought she couldn't keep me safe, and the fear that was driving her to run. Even though neither of our lives were ever like that again. I still remembered. And I never wanted to be in that position. No matter what you had, and the friends and family that were around you, someone bigger and badder might come in and threaten all that. The army seemed like a good place to start.'

'You wanted to learn how to protect yourself?'

Max shakes his head. 'I wasn't in danger anymore. My mom made sure of that. But other people in the world might be, and they might not have friends willing to risk everything, like my mom's friends did. I wanted to be that person who could come in and help.'

'That's a good back story to have, Max.'

'It's not a story, it's my life.'

'Every life is a story, Max. Some are just worth telling. Your mom got a good guy in the end.'

'My mom made her own life, Orchid. Sure, my dad was a part of that. But their life wasn't all LA sunshine and kisses. They were divorced for most of my life.'

'But they made it in the end.'

'Because family was more important to them than anything else. You're so caught up in your family having careers they cherish over a relationship with you that you're missing the point.'

'Which is?'

'Rich people can love their kids too, Orchid.'

I roll my eyes.

Max nods. 'You want a plot twist. My mom begged for a Vegas wedding the second time around.' He snorts. 'They had Elvis do the ceremony. Only a handful of people in attendance.'

'Well, I guess when you're in love, it doesn't matter.'

'A lot of things matter more than love. That one I learned from them. I saw them heartbroken over each other for twenty years, because some things got in the way of their love. Whatever happened to them was bigger than their love, and it won. So I get it. I get why you write your love stories and your romance novels. I get the big insta-love drama, because my mom spent my whole life telling me how she loved my dad the moment she met him. But I've also seen them hurt most of their lives because other important things got in the way.'

'Have you ever fallen in love?' I ask him.

'Yes.' He nods. 'But other things are in the way. Sometimes, you need the total package to make it work.'

'What's the total package?'

Max shrugs. 'They have to be on board with your whole life. The way you live day-to-day, with your family and friends. The things you want to achieve in life.'

I nod. 'My parents are like that. I know I give off the impression that I hate their career choice, but they are a good match for each other. They both wanted the same level of fame and success, and they drove each other to get it.'

'That's a good thing. Everything is a good choice in life, as long as it matches what both parties want.' He looks down at the table and I sense the tone changing.

'Is that what happened to you? Why you're not with this person you were in love with?'

'I don't think she would like my whole package, my whole family and work life. And that's a shame because I kind of love my life.'

I think I kind of love Max's life too.

'Want to know the worst thing about being a celebrity kid?' I ask him.

'Enlighten me,' Max says.

'The quirky names. In LA it's not so bad, everyone has quirky names. But sometimes I wish I was called something regular and old-fashioned.'

'Like Molly?'

I smile. 'Exactly like Molly.' I lean forward. '*Molly* gives me freedom to be the person I always wanted to be, to explore jobs and lives I'd never get to have as Orchid Rock. My first year here, I took a job at the store in town at my house. I got to know people, and they welcomed me into the town. I still know them all, and it's nice walking around, knowing that my neighbours are friendly.'

'I noticed. You know a lot of people in the village. But they think you're Molly.'

'I am Molly. I'm the same person, no matter what my name is, but the freedom of making up my own history is the thing I love. Do you know what the name Orchid means?'

Max shrugs. 'It's a flower, an expensive beautiful flower, and if you don't look after them, they die.'

I purposely wait until he takes a sip of his water before I tell him. 'It means testicle.'

Max chokes on his drink and I laugh.

'No, it doesn't,' he says.

'I swear to god.' I make a cross over my heart. 'My sophomore boyfriend's friends found out and he dumped me in the middle of homeroom. Said there was no way he was going to date a girl named Testicle Rock, no matter how rich her daddy was.'

Max stops laughing. 'That's a shitty thing to do to someone.'

I nod. 'Yeah, and a lot of people got a good laugh out of it for almost a full month.'

When the cheque comes, I reach out, but Max snatches it from the table and hands his credit card to the waitress.

'No, you can't pay,' I whisper and look around the restaurant so no one overheard. 'I can't have you buy me dinner here.'

'Right, but I was the one who just got paid this whole time to sit and eat.'

The stab of pain hits me in the heart. Of course, he's only here because he's working. Why else would he be having dinner with me? I forget he has a duty to follow me around and make small talk with me. To keep me company. I recover my faded smile quickly, but I see the look of regret on his face, and he's caught the hurt he accidentally placed there with that one line.

He's shaking his head. 'I didn't mean it like that.'

My blasé attitude to my sucky love life is something I've spent years faking well. 'No, not at all. I know exactly what you mean,' I joke. 'I need to start paying my dates to stick around longer than a month, right?

'It's not a bad idea, really. I mean, this has been the best date I've had in a long time, and it wasn't really a date.' I lean forward and keep the easy tone we've had all night. 'I wrote a book once about a woman who used an escort service. I could totally research the fuck out of finding a discreet service in the area.' I wink, but I don't get back a sarcastic comment or a cheeky grin I'm used to.

'I'm not sitting here because I'm getting paid, Orchid.'

I nod. 'I know, Max,' I lie.

Max stands and holds his hand out to me. 'Come on, I want to take you to meet my cousins.'

'Eh, you said your parents were only children.'

'They are. But my mum and dad's best friend's wife's brother's kids live ten minutes away. We spent a lot of time over the summer breaks together growing up.'

'Your who?'

He laughs. 'They live in Skerries.' He checks his watch. 'I'll text them to meet us at the harbour. Some ice cream and a walk along the beach sounds like something you might just need.'

I take a deep breath. 'I don't know. I might need a drink to meet your parents' best friends…'

'Wife's brother's kids.'

'Exactly. I've never been introduced to a guy's family before.

chapter thirteen

Orchid

After the walk around Skerries Harbour and sitting outside for drinks with Max's cousins, I'm freezing when we get home. Max has the fire lit and I've changed into my sweater and slipper socks and wrap a blanket around me in front of the TV.

'Want to watch some reality TV with me?' I ask.

'Seriously?' Max sits on the other couch. 'I thought you hated all reality shows.'

'I do, but the British baking ones are pretty good. I have four episodes to catch up on. Come on, it's torturous watching all the good food being baked when we can't have any.'

The entire house has warmed up with the fire by the time I go to bed, and I strip off to a vest and crash into bed. It's only a few minutes before I get up to brush my teeth and pee and right when I'm about to sit down, I realise there's no toilet paper here.

Shit.

I make a run for the downstairs bathroom and throw the door open to Max's naked ass, standing by the sink.

'Oh my god,' I yell while I pull the door closed. 'I'm sorry,' I shout through the door.

A few seconds later, Max pulls the door open, and he's wearing shorts. His hair is wet like he's just showered, and the steam follows him out of the bathroom.

'All yours,' he says, but his gaze roams my body and his face reddens as he takes in my attire.

We're both half naked. Or half dressed. Depends on whether you're an optimist or a pessimist, I guess.

99

I don't know what comes over me, but damn, do I want his body pressed against mine. He's all hard muscles and smooth skin, and I know the feel of his hands and body on mine will stop the itching underneath my skin.

I step forward into his space and lean up to his mouth. His hands wrap around my waist and find the patch of naked skin between my skimpy vest and the cotton panties.

He opens his mouth and lets me chase his tongue.

Chills run over my body and before I know it, my nipples are hard and I'm pressing against him for the heat.

I breathe out Max's name and try to claw my way back inside his mouth. He tastes too good not to keep this up.

Max fists my hair in his hand and slight pressure pulls my head back from his. Looking at me, he says. 'Now that's a damn good kiss, Orchid.'

He lets my hair go, and the lack of pressure has my head fall forward back to his mouth, while his hands fall under my ass, around the cotton line of my panties. Max picks me up and carries me to his downstairs bedroom.

Holy shit.

We're only inside the threshold of the door when he places me on the ground. I don't even think about it when I drop to my knees and reach for his shorts.

'Shit, Orchid.'

'That's what I was going to say.' I kiss his stomach and run my nose over the hair below his belly button.

'Maybe we shouldn't do this.' Max holds my hands and stops them from their perusal.

I stop. 'That's not what I was going to say.'

Max drops to his knees next to me and leans his forehead against mine.

'Why are you thinking so much about this?' I ask. 'Two people who are attracted to each other and need to release this sexual tension should just go with the flow.'

'The flow's going to take you all the way to my bed, Orchid, and I won't want to let you go after that.'

I close my eyes.

'Doesn't sound too bad to me.' I lean in and kiss Max's lips, but he's not responding like he did before.

'Someone once told me a kiss isn't worth a damn if the other person is merely tolerating it.'

Max grabs hold of my arms tight. 'That's not what this is. Things are complicated for me right now.'

'Wait, do you have someone at home waiting for you? Oh my god.' I look down at his hand for a ring I know isn't there. 'Are you married?' I shriek.

'No, Orchid, I don't have anyone. I'd be a pretty shit person if I did.'

'Oh.' I relax. 'Then what's the complication that's throwing ice over me right now?'

The smash from the kitchen makes me jump, but it makes Max stand at attention. There is a tone in the air, and I know it's not as simple as something falling. It sounded like a window being busted open.

'Lock the door behind me.' He reaches under the bedside cabinet and pulls out a gun.

'Was that there the whole time?' I hiss.

'The door, Orchid. And get on the floor.' He closes the door behind him, and I lock the tiny snip that's not going to do any good and sit my almost bare ass on the cold hardwood floor.

I can hear Max moving around the rooms downstairs, and I want to go out to him, but fear keeps me where I am. Max is a professional. I'd only get in his way. I keep telling myself the mantra to make myself feel better about not trying to help him, keep him safe, be his backup if he needs it, and curse myself for not bringing my phone down here and look around for Max's walkie-talkie or phone so I can ring Cameron outside.

There's a loud thud, and I can hear someone struggling.

Fuck.

I'm on my feet pacing the bedroom, and I know I should go help Max.

'Orchid,' Max calls. 'You can come out.'

101

I unlock the door and peek my head out. 'Max,' I whisper. Scared to move too far. 'What the hell is going on?'

'Backup is on the way, but we have him,' Cameron calls out and moves towards me.

I throw the door open with indignation. 'Have who?' I yell.

A few feet away, on the kitchen floor, near the dividing line to my office, is Archie. His back is pinned under Max's knee, hands bound in a tie wrap and struggling to move.

'I knew you had to be fucking her too,' Archie shouts to Max. 'That's all that family is worth.'

Max puts pressure on Archie's back and the tension in his taut arms collapses and he gives up his fight. There's no way Max is letting up.

'Get dressed,' Max says. 'The Gardai will be here in a few minutes.'

It's a full day before the interview and evidence are collected from my home. Forensics and scene of the crime officers have spent hours collecting glass fragments and fingerprints from the kitchen and the outside of the home. Max and Cameron were held for hours going over their involvement in my home and the restraint of Archie, and a full interview about our relationship and its violent ending was gone over and over until I felt dizzy with tiredness.

Ailish was even brought in at the request of Max to hand over her phone and laptop to forensics to analyse her activity on my social accounts and recover the deleted content that she's been taking down from my accounts.

And once it's all over and Max and Cameron are back at my house, I think I'm going to get a breather, but that only starts their own debriefing with their team.

I listen in from my office, typing nonsense on my keyboard, pretending I'm working, when I'm really listening to their accounts of what happened.

They have someone, an admin assistant maybe, taking notes of their account, and their relay of the information that they found out about the additional threats that Ailish has been unwittingly deleting for the past year. In her defence, I told her I didn't want to know any of the nasty stuff she was reading through, and to delete and block accounts. There's no way in hell I would have thought anything was ever going to come from it.

But Archie is spitting in his interview about being paid to mess with me, and how he needs extra money for fucking me. I felt the vomit roll around my stomach and up my throat when the Gardai told me about his interview. About how they are holding him on domestic violence charges since we used to date. And are looking for psych referrals too. But are concerned, along with my security team, about the possibility that someone else is orchestrating an attack on me.

Honestly, hearing it all, I just want to go home. And for the first time in a while, home feels like where my family is.

I pick up my phone and call my dad.

It's two more days before we're ready to go home a few days before our scheduled Thanksgiving visit. After Archie's arrest and trying to stop the complete anger and irritation at having someone like that in my home, I finally agree with my brain to shut out the whole incident and pretend that Archie never even existed.

Part of me can't wait to get out of here for a break and to let Max have the time off with his family that he needs, and for me to crawl into my old bed and pretend that nothing bad has happened the last while. But the irritation underneath my skin is brewing into a possible explosion at what arguments I might go home to.

I have a carry-on size bag packed with my laptop and notes folder sitting next to the bedroom door, when Max comes in without knocking. I'm ready way earlier than needed, but I always like to be packed, so I have the spare hours to tidy the house and have it ready for my return.

I spin around but am silenced when I see his serious face.

'Change of plan,' he says. 'There was an incident with the jet this morning before it left LA.'

'What kind of incident?'

103

His tone is too serious for a run-of-the-mill problem.

'I've booked a commercial flight out of Belfast, so we're going to have to drive.'

'Belfast? Why can't we fly out of Dublin?'

'We have to switch in London, and there might be a layover, so pack anything else you might need for a delay.'

'What the hell is going on? There might be a layover? There either is or there isn't?'

Max sighs. 'There was a security breach on the plane. Someone was stowed away in the food delivery assigned to the jet.'

'What?' I sit down on the edge of the bed.

'The crew saw them when they were readying the plane. Don't worry, though, there's no way my security team wouldn't have found them, even if they made it onto the jet.'

'Who were they? What the hell did they want?'

Max shakes his head. 'We don't know. We never caught them. There was no security, and they got away. But we have a backup plan to get you safely home.'

'Why commercially?'

'The jet has been grounded along with everything scheduled to go on it, and the crew. We're not taking any chances. I've booked six commercial flights for us home today, four out of Dublin and two out of Belfast, changing in London. That way, if this was a rouse to force us onto a commercial flight, there's no way to know which one we'll be on. I've a buddy from the service in the UK who's going to meet us in Belfast and accompany us home.'

He holds out two sheets of paper in front of me. 'Pick one.'

When I take the sheet of paper on the left, he offers me another three sheets, 'and one of these.'

I take the second sheet and my insides tremble.

'Congratulations, you just randomly chose our schedule home. We need to leave in one hour.' He nods and leaves me in a quiet room.

chapter fourteen

Orchid

On the Belfast to London route, I'm sandwiched in an economy seat between Max and his friend Cameron. In any other circumstances, I'd see the potential in writing a whole book series about these two young hot soldiers who save the day in private security, after fighting for their country, but today, I just want to stop the internal shakes. I can't even make a joke with Max about being on a low-cost airline, in economy, although it looks like this whole plane is economy. Max's and Cameron's legs are too long and both of their knees are touching the seat in front of us. The back row that we occupy is so tightly situated against the wall of the restrooms that there is only about an inch that the seats recline. I pretend to be cold and rub my arms to cover the shakes of my legs, and bounce my feet for some theatrics. 'Should have brought a sweater,' I say to no one.

'It's a quick flight,' Max says. 'Once we're in Heathrow, we have a thirty-minute dash to switch terminals and we're straight on the next leg.'

He moves his foot towards mine, and the simple feel of it is grounding. I stop bouncing my feet and try to take deep breaths in and out.

The deplaning and speed walking around Heathrow distracts me enough that I don't have to deal with anxiety about what awaits me in LA. I'll just have to keep working on the plane, or get drunk and watch some crappy comedy to keep me out of my head.

The first-class seat on the British Airways flight is a bed, and as soon as I sit down, I feel the tension in my back and shoulders dissolve and sink into the leather. I'm not sure how the other airline got away with selling those hard back upright things as 'seats'. No wonder people get stressed with travel. The entire journey for economy tickets is full of uncomfortableness in a tight space.

Cameron is sitting behind me, and Max's empty seat is to the left. Boarding is complete and the doors are closed when Max returns from the front of the plane with a blanket and hands it to me.

'Thank you,' I say.

He nods and leans over the seats, conversing with Cameron.

Once settled in his seat, he turns to me. 'So, tell me, what has you so nervous about going home?'

'I'm not nervous,' I lie.

'Your anxieties are spiking, and I know you well enough to know that unfortunately, the break-in at the house and the intruder in the jet aren't to blame.'

'I don't have anxieties.' I shake my head. 'I just overthink and worry about how things might be sometimes.'

'Like what?'

'Well, now, there are the attacks coming at me from my family's stalkers. But mostly, if there will be more arguing about me moving home. If they're going to ask me to be in the show for their new contract, or a Thanksgiving special or a Christmas end-of-year wrap-up. Sometimes I wonder if my refusal causes them problems, or if they lose money. They thought they might get with the whole family involved.'

I look at my hands when I say, 'I feel guilty for not being a part of their lives that way.'

'But you don't want to work on the TV show,' Max says.

'I know, but I feel like they want me to. And I wonder if I'm being a hypocrite by selling my life in the book world instead. I said I never wanted to live like them, but in a way, I do—just not on the same scale.

'Plus, I'm worried about my family and their crazy-ass stalker. What might happen to them.'

'Apparently, you had your own stalker too,' Max says.

I shake my head. 'No, that was a psycho ex who got jealous for no reason and thought he had a right to break into my house.'

Max tilts his head.

'Not no reason,' I correct myself. 'There was reason to be jealous of you. I just mean he had no claim over me.'

'Orchid, we need to talk about the other night.'

I straighten. 'Uh-oh, that never ends well,' I joke, trying to get a laugh out of Max and see that this conversation isn't going in the direction I think it is. It doesn't work. Max has his serious face on.

'I'm sorry if I crossed the line, Max. I genuinely thought it was a two-way thing and—'

'No, stop,' he says. 'Don't take it back,' he whispers. 'That's not what this is. It is a two-way thing. It's just complicated with who I am. We need to have a longer conversation, and right now'—he nods to Cameron behind him—'we don't have privacy.'

I look around the seat at Cameron, who is looking at nothing and everything all at once.

'He can't hear us,' I say.

Max tilts his head and Cameron answers, 'Yes, I can.'

I close my eyes, slightly mortified, and turn back to Max.

'I have a lot of work I need to concentrate on.'

I look at his laptop. 'Job hunting already?'

'No, my client was attacked twice in two days. I need to be on this. I'm sorry, but affairs of the heart need to wait while I do my job and keep you safe. I can't be distracted right now.'

'Affairs of the heart? How very British of you. And I'm fine. I'm sure it's all ironed itself out by now.'

Max shakes his head. 'Regardless, when we land, Cameron is going to take point on your security.'

'Why?'

'It's normal practice after a long rotation. I had a team lined up in LA to integrate you in with your parents' security, but Cameron is my personal favour, and I'm glad I pulled him in after the other night.'

'Oh, Max, don't tell me the kiss was that bad.' I wink.

Finally, Max laughs and goes back to his screen. 'We're going to talk, Orchid. Once we land and I officially sign off, we need to have a talk about this.'

I've only dozed for two hours, tossing in the seat and never getting as comfortable as I usually do. I could do with my home comforts when I've had a stressful day to help keep me asleep. A weighted blanket is the best thing to stop me from feeling like I have adrenaline running through me that needs to be expelled. Lavender mist machine, my eye mask—one that's padded and has beads built in to retain the essential oils. Meditation music, salt lamps, heck, even one of those things would help right about now. It's all too much to travel with, and why I only ever spend a couple of days at home when I need to.

I toss the cover off my body and it gets tangled in my feet. I can't stand the feeling of my feet being restrained, and the feeling causes my skin to itch over my entire body. I take a deep breath and try to forget about it all. The seat is reclined the whole way back, and without having to move, I open the privacy screen a few inches and see Max sitting upright in his seat, his laptop still open. Although, to the average person, he looks like he is working, I've seen that tension in him a million times. Every morning when we work out, every time I tried to pounce on him, and see if I could catch him off guard. Max isn't working like the businessman he's portraying. He's tense and ready for a fight. He's on guard and protecting me mid-air on a random flight that was chosen from a list of many that were booked under our names.

When we land and deplane, it feels a little overkill when Cameron steps up and ushers me out of the plane. Max trailing a step behind. Two security men meet us with a car and in a blink of commands and fast walking, followed by some fast driving, I'm out of the airport before I've had time to adjust to the temperature change.

'All a little dramatic, don't you think?'

Max is sitting in the back with me, while Cameron is driving and following the lead car out of the airport.

'We had some more information uncovered while we were in the air. In Archie's arrest statement, he admitted to vandalising your gate. I don't know if he's serious or playing the crazy card, but he said he was hired to date and spook you by someone in America.'

'What else?' I ask him. 'I know your pausing face, like you should tell me more, but you don't want to.'

'Mostly, he was mad about how he needs to be paid more for fucking you. That you didn't give it to him as much as he expected or was promised. He's not giving up his "employer" but he said he was given money to date you, with the intention of playing mind games against your family.'

'That motherfucker,' I shout. 'You know, he wasn't even good in bed,' I say to Max and Cameron. 'Like, a medium-sized dick that he didn't even know how to use.'

I groan out some anger and frustration and feel better about bad-mouthing him.

'He thought since it wasn't his idea, that the charges might be dropped. They're not, by the way. But since fucking with someone's head isn't illegal, they couldn't get any other charges on him.'

I lean my head back on the headrest and sigh. 'Is there more?'

'The stowaway on the jet in LA left behind a gun at the scene. Looks like it was dropped on the run.'

'Someone was coming to kill me?' I sit up and look at Max.

Max nods. 'That would be my professional opinion. The team is working through some other possibilities around kidnapping and ransom, or hostage and assault scenarios. But yes, I think they were trying to hurt you.'

'Why?'

'I don't know, Orchid.'

'I'm the least valuable person in the whole family. Why come after me?'

Max looks me in the eye, astounded by what I said.

'Oh stop. It's true. Do me a favour. I know you'll want to come in and look around my parents' house, but don't hang around, okay?'

'Well, there's an invitation if I've ever heard one.'

109

War *and* books

I shake my head. 'My family is crazy, and I don't want you exposed to them for too long. I want you to at least think I'm from something normal for another little while.

'People with money can be egotistical and eccentric. I don't want them quizzing you on your whole life and asking really awkward questions about minimum wage and how people survive on food stamps.

'I'm not making that one up. My sister actually asked that of one of my brothers' girlfriends in high school. And she wasn't being mean. She genuinely thinks if you live below Westwood, then you must be in a whole other world to her fairy tale.

'And all that was before that stupid TV show with that stupid studio.

'Don't even get me started with the Wembridge studio execs. They're always poking around as well, you know. Disguised as friends and wanting to *catch a beer with the old man*, but any time an exec comes sniffing, it's usually to up the drama to up the ratings. Which bleeds out off camera and before you know it, bam, we have a family drama happening off screen too. I don't want you to associate anything negative you see with them, with me. Does that make sense?'

'Sure thing, I'll take my minimum-waged soldier ass straight out of there.'

'That's not what I mean, Max, and you know it.'

'But if I was a rich boy, you wouldn't mind me hanging around them, but you wouldn't want to date anyone who had the same lifestyle and upbringing as your family? Got to say, Orchid, for someone who wants to avoid the LA drama, you certainly know how to create some of your own.'

'That doesn't matter, Max. You came here for a vacation and to see your parents. So, drop me off, leave me in the capable hands of your team, and go recharge.'

After Thanksgiving lunch the next day, there is a lot of activity at my parents' house. Their new security team walks the perimeter and Cameron is around the house, with another man I don't know, but have taken to be in charge of my parents' security.

After seeing my sisters and brothers and all the kids and eating lunch, it's almost 7:00 p.m. when I find time to call Max.

My mom has made up my old room for me, rather than staying in the pool house like I did when I was a teenager living here. There was a comfort to coming home to your childhood room. The memories of being in here when I was small, playing with toys and fighting with my sisters. But the sheets are fresh and smell like home, and the comforter is thick and fluffy. The bed is enormous and I crawl in with aching bones and tiredness and crashed adrenaline. I pull up the weighted blanket around me that was waiting in the room when I arrived yesterday. I know my parents don't know I have one of these at home, but when I asked them, Mom said that the security team had dropped it around for my arrival. Max is the only one I know who would have ever thought to have one waiting for me.

I find my phone. I've a missed call from two hours ago from Max and it makes me smile. Unless something was wrong. Shit, what if something was wrong?

I hit the redial button, and he answers on the second ring.

'Hi.' He breathes down the phone.

I smile when I greet him. He has his relaxed tone.

'Hope I didn't interrupt your family dinner,' I say.

'No, we're done. My mom made a big fuss of having her boy home. It's the first one in a while.'

I smile, glad that we made the trip in the end. 'That's good to hear.'

'I thought you might want to know that I was thinking of assigning someone new to your case.'

'What? Why?'

'Well, I kind of wanted to ask you on a date, and I can't really do what when I work for you. So, since we're in LA, technically on vacation, I thought I would officially take the week off and ask you out.'

'Okay,' I say. 'Is this why you wanted to sort out things before we talked on the plane?'

111

'And, Orchid. There's a lot you don't know about me, and partly that's my fault. I know you don't mean things personally when you go off on one, but I kept you in the dark about some things in the beginning, and the more I got to know you, the more I worried you wouldn't like the things about me.'

I sit up straight in the bed. 'That's ridiculous, Max. What would I possibly not like about you?'

'I'd rather speak to you in person, Orchid. It's going to be a big deal for me, and I don't want to do it over the phone.'

'It's not like you've killed someone, Max. Don't be so dramatic.'

There's silence on the other end of the phone.

'Shit, did you kill someone?' I hiss.

'Well, I mean technically… That's not what I was worried about, Orchid, but I was a soldier and I'm not even supposed to answer that question, but maybe you can make assumptions since I was injured in active gunfire.'

'Shit, I mean, well, yeah, I suppose I kind of knew that. Is that what you need to talk about? Because I can be an ear to listen if you need to talk to someone.'

'Thank you, but I've talked to the army shrinks about all that. I'm doing okay.'

I sigh in relief. 'Wait, did you kill someone more recently then?'

'What? No, Orchid. Christ, this has nothing to do with killing people. Jesus.'

I laugh. 'Well then, Max, let's make a date and we can get to know all the things we never got to learn about each other.'

'Okay, but I'm supposed to ask you on a date,' he says. 'How about the day after tomorrow? I'll pick you up and we can go for a hike?'

'Walking and talking sounds good.'

'And if you don't like what you hear, I already have you in the woods to hide the body.'

'Very funny, Maxy boy.

chapter fifteen

Orchid

I've been at Wembridge Studio's family cookout for five minutes before I spot Max drinking a beer alone in the corner of the room. It's exciting to see him a day earlier than planned.

Half the security team came with us to David Wembridge's house, while the rest stayed behind securing the property and doing god knows what. I guess until family death threats and break-ins stop, this will be the new normal around here. Thank god we only have a few more days left until I head back to Dublin.

I down my champagne in one go and leave the glass on the table by the bar while I make my way over to Max. I'm glad I dressed up, all of a sudden wanting to make an impression on him. And he smiles when he spots me walking towards him, but the smile quickly turns to confusion.

'So, you're finally drinking on your day off.' I nod at the bottle in his hand. 'How the hell did you get in here? Surely your own security company is checking invites at the door.'

'Your family is here?' Max asks.

'Of course. It's our first time, though. I'm normally in Dublin, and everyone else is doing their own thing. One part of being forced to stay at home by your team is that we actually had to spend more time together doing the family thing. And I have to say, the Wembridge house is pretty darn big and impressive.' I lean in. 'And his wife even has her own house across the street. Apparently, they live in one and use the other for entertaining.' I raise my eyebrows and look around for another drink.

Max looks over my shoulder at my dad, who is talking to David Wembridge himself only a few feet behind us. Shit, I never saw them there.

'Shit, do you think they heard me?'

I don't need an answer when my dad shouts my name and brings David Wembridge over with him.

My dad leaves me hanging when he hands me his glass of whiskey and says he'll be right back.

'David, do you know Max? He's head of my dad's new security team. Max, this is the host, David Wembridge. He owns and runs Wembridge Studios and, wait, you're a scientist as well, right?' I turn my full attention back to David. 'What field do you study?'

Max doesn't shake David's hand like I expect him to, and David gives him an awkward stare before he laughs.

'Oh, I forgot how complicated life was when you're twenty-five.'

'Excuse me?' I ask.

'Enjoy the party, Orchid. It was nice to finally meet you.' David raises his glass to me in salute and disappears into the crowd of the room.

'We should really go talk, Orchid. The hike tomorrow was actually a stupid security risk, so I guess there is no time like the present. Unless you're drunk. Then maybe we should wait.'

'I've had one drink, Max, I'm not drunk. Although you look like someone ran over your kitten. Why the hell do you look so miserable?'

Someone clinks a glass, and the room quiets down.

'Oh, Christ,' Max says, not even trying to be quiet or discreet.

'Shh,' I admonish him. 'What's with you? You're never this rude.'

David Wembridge is standing near the patio doors, glass in hand, waiting for the room to quiet.

Max leans over my shoulder. 'We can sneak out now, Orchid. No one will ever notice.'

I tilt my head. 'I may talk a lot of shit, Max, but these people are actually nice. And they invited me here and we can't drink their alcohol and not even stick around. Have some class.'

My dad holds out his hand to usher me over with the rest of the family, and I take a step forward. When I'm embedded in between my sisters and my parents, my brothers flanking the Rock family ensemble and keeping the kids occupied, I listen to David Wembridge talk about his thanks for his family and his extended family that he's worked with the last twenty years.

When I turn around, Max isn't alone anymore.

Stella Lewis, David's wife and a formidable businesswoman in her own right, of all people, has snuck into my spot and is talking to him. I'm struck first by her sheer beauty and elegance, the way she stands and carries her confidence. She leans in and kisses Max on the temple, sneaking her arm around his back to give him a small squeeze. At the back of the room, no one can see them well. Except me, who can't take my eyes off them.

It all makes perfect sense now. Why Max is even here. The look of contentment and love between the two, not a care in the world who might see them at the back of the room, giggling and making fun of the host and his long assed speech.

They look so alike I don't know why I never noticed before.

Max is Stella Lewis and David Wembridge's son.

chapter sixteen

Max

Cameron makes eye contact with me from across the room and nods towards the hallway. I leave my beer with Mom and move out of the conservatory and around the side hall to meet Cameron in the front reception space.

'I know you're off this case and normally I wouldn't come to you with this while you're on rest.'

'What is it?' I ask Cameron.

Technically, he's saved my ass from a fight with Orchid. When she spotted me with my mom, and it took her all of three seconds to piece the puzzle together. I could see the wheels turning behind her eyes as she figured out my secret that I was too chicken to tell her beforehand. I'm a trust-fund LA rich kid, parents who can afford two Beverly Hills houses—one to live in and one to entertain in, as Orchid put it. And I'm everything she's run five thousand miles to escape.

'It's with Orchid's social media accounts. It looks like there have been threats coming in that we didn't know about.'

I lead Cameron into the downstairs office.

Cameron closes the door behind him. 'I don't want you stressing out, but I know your relationship here has crossed some line.'

'She's an adult. And we haven't crossed any lines.'

'She's a client. And the way you were talking on the plane, you almost crossed lines, and you're stepping back from her primary care team.'

I nod.

'It's a good decision. It's hard to work properly if feelings get in the way. Having someone else there with her—with you two—if you become a thing, will only help protect her even more. And it looks like she needs it.'

My head snaps up to attention. 'What's happened now?'

'I took over some admin roles that you had on her social media and there were a bunch of pending posts that looked suspicious. Semi-threatening, angry, and one even hinted towards her duping people about who she was. I interviewed her assistant on the phone this morning,'

'Ailish,' I say, and he nods.

'She filled me in on things she has been deleting from the main pages and some things that haven't made it live due to admin changes they made recently. She doesn't remember everything and knows there were multiple accounts that looked suspicious. We had IT in the Irish security company you hired run analysis on her computer and phone and see what we could get.

'Seven new social media accounts that were doing most of the abusive talking were tied back to one IP address here in LA. We handed the info over to the police this afternoon. Just waiting to see if it fits into any of the attacks on her family.'

'So this might not be purely to do with the Rock family? It might all be to do with Orchid?'

'Maybe.' He nods. 'You know how these stalker things can get super specific and obsessive for apparently no reason.'

'Could be that someone has it in for Orchid and has been targeting her family, trying to get to her through them.'

Cameron nods. 'We might have had the full attention on the wrong members of the family.'

'Where is she now?' I stand up, adrenaline fuelling me, and fear at not having eyes on her.

'Most of the team is here.' Cameron holds his hand out, blocking me from storming through my house looking for her. 'She's safe. But she'll be safer back home with the full team and her family. You should come too if it will make you feel any better. But there's a reason why you put this team together in this company.'

I let out a deep breath. 'Because we get the job done.'

He nods. 'Don't freak out and try to take her somewhere else. It's the first thing you'd advise against if this was a regular client.'

I tap Cameron on the arm. 'Thanks, man.' I open the door and walk back out through the hallway, back to the party. 'We should make you point on this job when we get back to Ireland. You okay to work a few months on this if needed?'

Cameron nods. 'I can give you six weeks. I have some things happening that I need to be back in England for. The sooner the better. But six weeks will help you get a secondary team set up if you need it longer.'

'Let's hope this comes to a head soon, then.'

Cameron and I stop at the entry to the kitchen and look out at the Thanksgiving party.

Orchid is standing next to her family, chatting to one of her sisters. Her brother is sitting next to her, and her parents are hovering around the table near them, chatting to other couples. I scan over the guests. Everyone here I know. My family and extended family and their kids. Some people from my parents' work. And my security team around the perimeter and near the Rock family. All is exactly where they need to be. My eyes land back on Orchid, and all I want to do is go to her, be there with her and in that family circle, laughing and being a part of her life, like I have been these past months.

'You think she's going to invite you home to live with her?' Cameron asks.

'What?' I look at him.

'When you assign me as the new head, there's no need for you to come too. Not unless you're there as a boyfriend or whatnot.'

I let out a sigh. I forgot all about that. I've no real reason to go back and live in Orchid's house. Or the cottage. To hang out with her every day. I can't put myself back on the case just because I want to be near her. The only logical thing I could do is move nearby and see if this relationship could go anywhere. Now I sound like a stalker.

'Maybe you should just work on getting her to forgive you first.'

'Forgive me?'

'Dude, I was travelling with you guys for one day. You never told her who your family was.'

'She has a lot of issues with rich families and the LA life,' I tell him. 'She ran away to try to have a simpler life with no drama.'

'Well, that didn't work out well for her then, did it? Maybe all she needs is to see the Wembridges together. I have to admit, I was shocked when I found out who your family was too. Until you meet you guys together—you're just as normal and fucked up as everyone else.' He laughs at his own joke.

'There's no other family than mine that's so heavily embedded in the entertainment industry. My dad owns the network that her family work for. My mom is an agent. My uncle'—I point to Mike and his wife, Audrey, who are sitting around the pool loungers with their kids—'is an action hero actor that she makes fun of for earning too much money.'

'Isn't she worth the try?'

I look him in the eye. 'She sure is.' I nod and take off toward the Rock family.

When I make it over to Orchid, I know it won't be a simple escape with her to a private conversation. I've not seen her brother since high school, and he'll want to chat. Her parents will probably want to see if there are any updates with Archie in Ireland and god, her sister—her sister tried to make out with me the last time I met her at a network party.

Instead of being polite and having all the conversations I'd rather not have right now, I reach over to the side of the sofa Orchid is sitting on, interrupt everyone, and take Orchid by the hand. 'We need to have a chat.' I tug her hand and she rises out of her seat. 'I'll bring her right back when we're done.'

I don't let go of her hand when we turn and walk through to the back of the house. Instead, I tighten my grip on her, weave my fingers through hers, and run my thumb over the base of her hand. I tow her through the house and towards the staircase that wraps around the entranceway. I lead her to my bedroom and adjoining office.

It's ridiculous really. The size of this place, and Orchid was right, we do own the house across the street. After me and my mom moved here, my dad bought the second house so we could be close to each other. It meant I was never far from either of them. My gran still lives with us, and Uncle Mike and Aunt Audrey are only down the road. I remember when we lived in a three-bedroom apartment together, well before Mike married Audrey. But when my dad and Mike started working with my mom, they were all broke and living with us and my grandma. It was the only thing they could afford to get by in the careers they knew would take off eventually.

'You were wrong about one thing, Orchid,' I tell her. 'My dad's house is used solely for his work and research. He would rather die than have a party over there. Shocker, I know, but we live in the same house that we entertain in.'

I smile tightly at her and she looks abashed. She must be trying to remember every conversation she's ever had with me about the Wembridge clan. The Knight Wembridge and Lewis private jet, the reality TV station ruining lives and executives wanting more and more of her family's soul. Because that's what Orchid and her social anxieties do. She tortures herself with every iota of every conversation she's ever had, and she stresses until she feels nauseous about who she might have upset, and she frets until she nearly falls apart. Because she's a good person. She uses gossip and tidbits of information to help put the drama into her work—but deep down, she worries about everyone and everything.

I open my bedroom door and tug her inside. 'It's all right, Orchid. I didn't fully explain who I was, so you have nothing to feel bad about,' I tell her.

'Bad about?' she shrieks. 'I don't feel bad about anything.' She drops my hand and folds her arms over her chest. One foot out farther than the other, she's on a stand-off and she's pissed. Shit. Maybe I finally misread her.

'You lied to me.'

I take a step farther into my room, which is really more like a large studio apartment, and walk over to the couch and TV area.

Orchid looks around the room, which is really two rooms knocked into the one to make an overly large bedroom and living space.

'This is insane,' she says, looking over the place. 'It's bigger than the cottage you've been in.'

'Not quite,' I say. But it's pretty damn close.

I sit on the sofa and Orchid balances on the arm of the couch opposite me.

'When I came back from deployment after my injury, I spent a lot of time in my room. Healing from my injuries but also giving myself some head space to adapt to the loss of my friends on duty and the PTS that was hanging around with being shot up and nearly killed at the tender age of twenty-three. Cameron is still struggling, mostly because he believes his unit, the British unit that we were there to assist, was sabotaged internally. But that's a whole other story in its own right. Once I was home about a week, my mom had the wall between my bedroom and other room knocked down to give me more space. "If you want to live up here on your own, you can at least have space to put in a gym and a TV area," she said. Eventually, it worked. I got out of bed and could open the balcony doors and pretend I was in my own world. Exercise with views of the pool, shower and then move over to the living room area where I finally came up with the idea to create a new security business.

'My mom used to hang out up here with me for a while. I didn't love coming downstairs. The house would have people working in the downstairs offices, and the housekeeper, and I didn't feel like I could keep everything together in front of them. So my mom picked up her laptop and brought it up here.' I point to the sofa Orchid is perched on. 'It must have been uncomfortable after an hour or two, but she worked there as much as she could. Dad too. I think they took it in shifts to make sure I wasn't alone too much.'

'I had no idea things were that bad for you,' she says.

'No worse than others who manage to make it back alive. But I'm not telling you this to change the subject, Orchid. You're mad at me, and you have a right to be.

'Look at what I grew up with. I'm everything you hate, and the thought of you hating me as much as you hate everything to do with this part of your life killed me, even when I first met you. That's

121

why I kept it from you. And the reason I'm sharing my life's doom and gloom is that you need to know that money doesn't make or break a family.'

'But it can,' she whispers. 'Eventually, it broke my family and I don't think they even notice I'm gone. I don't want that for my future—for my kids.' She swallows a lump in her throat and moves to sit on the sofa.

'I know this is crazy because we're not even a thing yet. But all of a sudden I'm worried about this changing things with us. What if we get married and have kids, and they are brought up with two parents who are chasing careers instead of making the kids a priority? I wanted to live a life where I was comfortable and happy, but I was never chasing to keep earning more and more. And I've got that place.'

'And you don't want your partner to be chasing the dream every day.'

'Chase your dreams, but don't choose the dollar and the dreams in front of the kids.'

She lowers her head. 'I know this is a conversation that's totally hypothetical and will probably scare any man off.'

'But it's important,' I tell her. 'Your family values and what you want out of life and family should be a conversation to have before things get too deep.'

She nods. 'I always thought I had earned enough, that when I met someone, I would be happy to slow down or retire early, and that there would be no pressure on either of us to work like my parents did. But, Max, if this is what you come from, how will you ever be content with a simple life? You'll always be chasing to earn as much as your parents did, to live in a home this size, and I can't play second best again.

'I don't want someone who will put me second over making another million in one year.' She stands up and makes for the door. 'And worst of all, I'm scared that if I get sucked back into this life'—she moves her hand around the room—'when things go wrong, like they have this week—I'm happy to run back home to my family. Because I love them, and I want to be near them. And it's obvious that their money and their security can offer me what I need at a time like this.

Which just scares me more—more that I need to be just like them to survive. That I might have to keep pushing my career to the level they did. That deep down, their success is something I've been brought up with and something I'm chasing, too. I'm scared I'll end up loving my career and making money more than I'll love my kids.'

'Can't you have both?' I ask her.

She shakes her head. 'Not that I've ever seen. My parents were good people, Max. They just loved their careers that tiny bit more than me.'

'Come meet me tomorrow,' I tell her.

She turns to me. 'What for?'

'Because I'm not going to let you ruin this before it starts. Eight a.m., get Cameron to bring you over here. I'm going to show you what my *family values* are all about.'

chapter seventeen

Orchid

The worst thing about me is when the shit hits the fan, I overthink every conversation I've ever had with someone. Especially when you realise you fucked up. I take slow steps down the stairs as my legs shake. The last thing I need is to fall flat on my face.

Cameron is waiting at the bottom of the stairs, his face stoic and impassive as I reach him.

'Can you take me to my parents' house?' I ask him. I've been drinking, or I would drive myself. And I don't even know where I left my purse and I really don't want to walk back into the party to look for it.

I don't know what has me feeling worse—that I've been lied to, or duped, or that I've made so many assumptions about Max and the Wembridge family, and I've been wrong about them all. Or maybe it's that I've allowed myself to fall head over heels for someone and I didn't even know their full name.

Cameron leads the way down the drive, and the valet has the security cars lined up and ready to move out near the front. In the back seat, Cameron shuts my door and we're moving within a few seconds.

I never even told my parents I was leaving. Shit, and I have no phone to text on.

Staring out the window, I swipe away the tears of regret and take deep, steady breaths the entire way home.

All I've done since I met Max, in his dad's studio and then on his dad's bloody private jet, was bitch about the Wembridge family. *His* family. I can't even stay mad that he never told me who he was, but Christ—would I say anything if someone was so hell-bent on dissing *my* family in their tirade about the life they left behind.

I actually hide my life and family connections just as much as Max has hid his from me. I hide my whole life from everyone.

Why the hell didn't I just keep my mouth shut, and you know, ask Max for his surname?

The front driveway of my parents' house is imposing and impressive, even for Beverly Hills. The gates sweep open, inviting people into our home in an elegant open-arm gesture. That's what the realtor told us when we bought the place. The driveway winds up a small hill and Cameron turns the car around the waterfall feature in the driveway, stopping at the front door.

We exit the car together, and thank god, Cameron seems to have a key to the house and opens it up for me.

I walk past him, through the door, and instead of strutting the whole way to my bedroom, I pause at the bottom of the stairs. There's a crackling sound coming from the back of the house.

Cameron's noticed too, and he grabs my arm. 'Out.' He pulls at me, and as I'm being tugged through the foyer, I smell it.

'Is that fire?' I shriek.

I pull my arm loose. 'We need to make sure everyone's out.' I think back to the masses of people who are usually here on any given day. Assistants and office staff that run my parents' various ventures are usually in the downstairs offices. There is always at least one of the full-time housekeepers and a chef on hand. Not to mention the new security team and any amount of business personnel who might be in for a meeting. Or a makeup assistant or production crew, getting stills or recording filler content of the house or newly decorated rooms.

'It's Thanksgiving, Orchid. No one's here.' Cameron's Scottish accent is strong when he shouts. Actually, it's probably strong all the time. I just rarely hear him speak.

'Close the fire doors,' I tell him. 'There's an alarm I'm going to activate manually, just in case.' I run to the security panel behind the front door and push the panic buttons that sound alarms all over the house. Why the fire alarms haven't gone off already is a shit show.

'There should be sprinklers activated if the fire is in the kitchen,' I call out to him, making a run for the back of the house to see if the sprinklers can be set off, or if the fire's not too big, perhaps we can control it ourselves.

Under the stairs is a fire extinguisher that I unhook from the wall and run towards the kitchen. When Cameron makes a grab for me, I realise he's grabbing the extinguisher and I let him take it. Opening up the nozzle, he aims the tube in front of him, but the moment we turn the corner into the kitchen and see flames from the stove, over the counters, and the drapes, I'm pretty sure it's too much for just one extinguisher.

Cameron is spraying from a distance, and I duck around the back of him, into the pantry for another extinguisher. There's not one in here, even though the hook screwed into the wall means there should be one. I need to grab the phone and call the fire brigade, but when I move a step towards the door, I see the fire extinguisher as it rushes towards my head and clatters off the side. A shadow surrounding Sabrina's face is all I see behind the driving force as I fall backwards out of the pantry and hit the kitchen tiles as I fall.

I'm not unconscious. That's all I'm clinging onto as the pain in my head is so intense it makes me scream out to stop the vomit from the pain surfacing out my throat. The tiles are warm on the ground and I try to roll over, to get up off the burning floor, but I can't lift my head up. I'd rather be unconscious. Especially with the screaming. Someone is shouting my name, but I can only hear the edges of fuzzy syllables that I know collectively are my name. They are loud, but they are far away.

Pulling at my arms drags me into the fire and I scream. The smoke chokes me in half a second and no longer is lifting my head off the ground the problem, but breathing just became an issue.

Someone is dragging me closer to the fire, and the smoke is black and I can't see anything. I try to hit out, but the other person is still calling my name and coughing, too.

In a few seconds, I'm dragged, kicking and hitting and trying to hold my breath through the thickest smoke. Dumped in the hallway. Away from the thickest fog, the person helps me stand and I realise it's been Cameron this whole time. I can't tell him that someone attacked me. I can't speak at all, but he hitches an arm around my side and throws me over his shoulder, carrying me out to the driveway.

Two officers run out of the community police car that's sitting idle on the other side of the waterfall. Cameron places me softly on the ground, and I try to sit up. The two of us were only in there for a few minutes, yet our skin is charcoal, and our clothes hot and almost melted to our bodies. Sweat is running down me, and out in the cool air, I can feel the shivers start.

Cameron pulls his shirt over his head and places it on the throbbing side of my head.

'Hurt,' is all I can manage to say.

'You're bleeding.' Cameron moves to the side when one of the community police officers arrives with a first aid box and tries to find something to clean me up with.

Looking at the front door, the house looks normal. Like nothing at all unusual is happening on the inside. Expect for the alarm ringing, and the smell of Cameron and me, you would have no idea that the place is burning at the back.

Something cackles on the officer's radio, and Cameron tells him to go, while he takes over the first aid kit. The officer runs off, his gun raised, and circles the side of the building towards the backyard.

Cameron doesn't hang around. He lifts me up into his car and drives. I'm in the front seat next to him, my head spinning from side to side and I pat down my pockets, looking for my phone. My beeper fob is in my phone case. All I need to do is press it and Max will come for me. But I don't have it. I don't have anything.

My head feels like it's about to explode and I want to vomit out my entire insides. I lean forward to put my head between my legs, but I forgot to put on my seat belt when we got into the car. With the fast driving and the weight of my head, I fall right out of my seat and into the footwell.

'Orchid,' Cameron shouts.

I raise my hand in the air to let him know I'm okay, but I'm going to rest here. I really need to just sleep and get this headache gone.

Closing my eyes, I get flashes of the last few minutes replaying over and over again. And that's when I realise who smashed the fire extinguisher off the side of my head. It's bittersweet knowing that it was all about me. And not at the same time. And that now, there is nothing in the world I can do about any of it, except stay in the footwell of a car and let a practical stranger drive me away from everyone I love. So I sleep. I close my eye and if I happen to wake up, I'll deal with what comes next.

chapter eighteen

Orchid

My brothers, Ali and Elvis, are the first people I see when I open my eyes. Elvis is sleeping on the chair at the side of my hospital bed, and Ali is on the small couch, his head hanging over the top, and his feet dangling off the bottom.

Shit, I'm in a hospital. I gasp and sit up and my brothers startle awake with my movement.

'What's going on?' The rasp in my throat makes me groan and slowly sink into the bed.

Ali pours some water, while Elvis makes his way to the other side of my bed.

'That bloody psycho tried to kill you, that's what happened,' he says and his eyes dart to Ali, who stays silent, and hands me the glass.

'How are you feeling?'

'Where's Mom and Dad?' I kind of expected them to be here. 'Is everyone okay?'

Ali places a hand on my shoulder. 'Everyone is fine,' he says. 'I needed them to watch the kids 'cause I wanted to be here when you woke up.'

I nod and drink a small amount of soothing liquid and gasp out in relief when I lay my head back.

'This was always about me,' I say and my brother tenses.

Elvis sits on the side of the bed and Ali shifts next to me. He was never able to just stand still.

'What do you remember?' Ali asks.

'The fire and the bloody knock to the head. It was only when I was in the car with Cameron that I put it all together.'

'I'm sorry,' Ali whispers and Elvis shouts next to him.

'No. This is neither of you guys' fault. And this is not about Orchid or you, Ali,' he says. 'A psychopath who gets into our lives and tries to kill one of us'—he swallows down as he speaks—'is not our fault. It's her fault. She's the nut job,' he spits.

Ali nods. 'But I married her,' he says, and I can hear the croak in his voice. 'I always knew she had an obsession with Orchid, or a jealous thing, whatever. Even after high school, when we started dating, she always had a hang-up with you, Orchid. And I should never have kept dating her. But before I knew it—'

'She was up the duff and looking for a ring?' Elvis throws out and Ali nods.

'Stop it.' I take Ali's hand. 'I remember her smashing my head with the extinguisher and it all made some crazy sense. It's been her threatening us this whole time?' I ask.

'*My wife*'—Ali spits out—'was detained at the fire scene and taken into custody. We haven't heard anything else since. But it makes a weird sort of sense, doesn't it?' He tries to laugh and hide his tears.

'It really does.' I take his hand and am weirdly glad that he's now able to see through the evilness that's been driving its own wedge with his family and the Rocks. Sabrina, my high school friend, has been a different person since she started dating my brother ten years ago. Going from my best friend to someone I barely spoke to, to someone I never recognised anymore. And when I started writing and distancing myself from the family, she made it a point to distance us even more. I knew she was always stirring things behind my back, but I never thought it would get this far.

'Max Wembridge was here too,' Elvis said. 'But his security team rotated him out last night to get some rest. He asked me to give you this.' Elvis hands me a slip of paper wrapped around my phone and alarm fob. I let them tumble to the bed and open up the paper. One line is scrawled in the middle.

Don't forget, you owe me a breakfast date.

I laugh, and it vibrates pain through my chest, coughing until I catch my breath.

I'm released from the hospital the next day and put on bed rest for the week. My parents and I, along with Ali and his three kids, have all moved in with my sister Adhara, while the fire damage is being assessed. Just as well, Adhara, *the brightest star* of the family, has a huge-ass house that can accommodate us all. Because it looks like Elvis hasn't left, nor my other sister Coco. And between them all, they have six kids.

Cameron is back at work, with only smoke inhalation. He brushes off the concern when I try to hug him at Adhara's house. He's taken the lead on my security again, and since he saved my life, my parents are only too thrilled to have him and keep bringing him coffee and cookies.

It only takes two days of napping and watching TV, being bugged by my brothers and sisters, who take turns lounging around my room with me, before I text Max and ask to see him.

You cooking tomorrow morning? *I ask.*

He texts back straight away.

Hell yeah. You sure you're up to a visit?

I'm going crazy here. I need some normality.

And what? I'm the most normal person you know?

Strangely, yes.

131

chapter nineteen

Max

At 7:30 a.m. I make my way into the kitchen and start breakfast. Since I'm technically still on vacation, and I really need to take a break before I burn out on this one, I only did half of our sprint on the treadmill. Was easier that way than going for a run outside because I called Cameron first thing to get an update on any developments on Sabrina's arrest, and her connection to any of the other threats that have happened to the Rocks or Orchid in Dublin.

He was reluctant at first, but since I own the company and hired him, he was obliged to keep me updated on all cases.

And the update was fuck all. The team is still gathering information and to make an assumption at this time wouldn't be prudent. Fucker. I was the one who made that line up. It made me run faster. Harder and pissed off always works well for me in the gym.

Mom and Dad arrive at the breakfast table right before 8:00 a.m. and we fall into our usual routine. Dad's on coffee—he makes the best coffee and claims it's because he's a scientist and they put the most effort into the water coffee ratio and heat temperatures—but my mom swears it's just because he uses the expensive coffee. Gran is on juice and condiments and she takes her job seriously. Matching condiment sets that she refills the night before and makes sure the juice is sufficiently chilled and presented in a decorated ceramic jug that matches the season.

Mom is setting the table and I tell her to add a fifth place.

'For who?' she asks. 'You better not have had a girl stay over her, young man,' she mocks, but the doorbell goes off and I toss the dishtowel in her face while I answer the door.

Orchid is standing on my doorstep and I want to hug her and cry and squeeze her all at once. She doesn't even have a mark on her. I know from the security report that she had a cut on her right side, over her ear, but her hair must be covering it. She looks relaxed in yoga pants and a sweater. Hair tied back and her usual pale complexion before she's put her makeup on.

Cameron's a pace behind her and I open the door to invite them in. There is a car and driver parked in our drive, and Cameron returns to him to sweep the perimeter and they will probably take up positions at the front and back of the house. My house is secure. My dad's house is secure and so is Uncle Mike's. Those were my first jobs when I set up my new company. Nothing happens on this street without us knowing about it.

We talked on the phone for two hours last night while she told me how she was feeling and how her family has all moved into her sister's house. That's a lot of people with partners and kids and the full security team. But at least it's the full security in one place and things look like they are wrapping up on the threat level.

'Morning,' I tell Orchid when she steps inside the house, moving into her space and giving her a kiss on the cheek while I close the door behind her. She blushes, but she doesn't move away. In fact, she kind of softens into the kiss.

'Blushing looks out of place on you. Especially since the last time we kissed, you sank right to your knees.'

Her eyes widen and she tries to hold back her laughter and my dad clears his throat behind us.

Orchid holds her breath and closes her eyes, and I slowly turn around.

'I heard nothing,' he says.

'Max,' Orchid hisses behind me.

'Really wasn't what it sounded like,' I tell him, purely for Orchid's sake. No need to embarrass her before she's even in the door.

'Nice to see you again, Orchid.' Dad turns to me. 'Your mom is trying hard not to eat everything. Come on.'

133

War and books

Orchid looks at me while I nod and let Dad lead the way to the kitchen. I wait for Orchid and we walk together through the house and into the small nook in the kitchen, where we sit for family meals. With just the four of us, we never use the formal dining room unless Mom or Dad have a work dinner meeting, or Mike and Audrey are here with the kids—then we practically need to bring in soundproofing and a tent to keep everyone huddled in the one place.

Orchid stops on the threshold of the kitchen when she sees my mom and gran sitting at the table. Their whispered conversation halted at our arrival and I know my dad is making a face as he makes his way over to the table. The Rock family affairs have not only been a source of gossip for the neighbouring community and the news stations, but since the family work for my dad's production studio, there have been countless meetings and strategies for working the rest of the season and what they legally and morally can include in the episode due to air next month.

'Orchid, you know my mom, Stella. And this is my grandma, Pamela.'

Orchid doesn't falter when she makes her way over to shake their hands, and my gran shoos Mom and Dad closer together to make room for Orchid.

Once I sit down and hand Orchid a plate, my family takes their cues that no explanation is going to be offered, and they dig in as usual.

Breakfast is my meal. The one I love to cook. Setting up for the day is important, but for anyone who works a physical job, you need to get this one right. Eggs cooked three different ways, low-fat sausages, since it's technically a vacation, back bacon with the fat removed, grilled tomatoes and mushrooms, baked beans cause my dad's English and we were raised on beans and toast and fresh fruit and porridge—mostly it's just me who eats that—because there's nothing better than a two-course breakfast.

Once we're all eating, the conversation starts to flow. Gran starts, like she always does, by asking who's home for lunch and what we're going to have.

I look over at Orchid. 'The one thing you'll notice is that we love our food here. We're literally eating and we're already planning the next meal.'

She smiles. 'I did notice. But hey, if you all cook like Max, I don't blame you for loving the food.'

I chuckle. 'It's nice being home and not having to cook every meal.'

Orchid opens her mouth in shock. 'Hey, I can cook. I do cook. I've managed to survive many years on my own, thank you. You were the one who showed off his skills and stole the job.'

'How were you guys getting on in Ireland?' Mom asks, and the whole table knows it's a loaded question.

'Fine,' I tell her. 'I actually wanted Orchid to meet you guys today.'

Orchid looks over at my mom and back at me.

'Oh, why's that?' Mom asks.

'Things get busy around here, and I was telling Orchid how we always make time to have breakfast and dinner together.'

'And lunch,' Grandma says.

'Well, there's a reason some of us miss that one, Pam,' my dad says. 'I think the cooking genes skipped you.'

Mom laughs and Gran just scoffs and turns her attention to Orchid. 'If you're here all day, I usually make salad. Salmon salad was what was planned today. It takes a special kind of someone to screw up a salad, so you'll be in safe hands.'

Dad swallows his coffee. 'Don't make me tell the story about the time you set the kitchen on fire.'

'Oh god, please,' Mom shouts. 'You need to get over that one. It was twenty years ago.'

'It was a small fire.' Gran winks at Orchid before she realises what she's said and the whole table apologises.

'Don't be silly. Can't keep hiding from the fact my sister-in-law tried to burn down my house and leave me inside, now can we?' She smiles and lets the table settle.

135

War and books

'Well, we have work upstairs to do today, so we'll be here, Gran.' I interrupt. 'And Cameron and the driver will want to be fed too,' I say. She loves looking after people. Cooking, decorating. Anything she can do that's creative and satisfying.

The rest of breakfast is taken up with small talk and chat about Ireland. Gran's never been, but Dad has been for golf loads of times and tries to talk to Orchid about all the links courses in Dublin. Orchid has no interest in golf, but she nods along at the names of towns and places near her home.

When the conversation turns to her books, she shrieks when I tell them I read her books and they're great.

'You read my books?'

'Of course. What else was I going to do? I had to hang out in your social media all the time, so it was only fair I knew what those women were referring to.'

'Oh god,' Orchid moans and dips her head.

'What?' Gran asks. 'They're not full of sex, are they?'

Orchid laughs out loud. 'Oh, well.'

'Yes.' I nod and swallow down the last of my coffee.

'Oh, you can tell a lot about what sex books people read,' Gran says.

Orchid turns a deep red that I have to save her.

'Okay, we're all done here.' I hold out my hand and Orchid takes it as we get up from the table.

Dad's still chewing on toast when he says his goodbyes and we leave them to talk about us.

At the top of the stairs, along the hallway, instead of leading Orchid into my room, where we spoke yesterday, I open the door next to it. My office.

This was one of my gran's projects. As soon as she realised I was starting a company, she jumped into action. I didn't need an office, what with the gigantic bedroom that had been converted for me—or you know, the two houses that are basically mansions with multiple rooms in their own rights. But the guestroom next door became my workplace, which now means I have this whole side of the upper level to myself.

When we go inside, the tone here is so different from the room next door. Apparently, that's what Gran was going for. A clear distinction between work and rest spaces.

This room is bright and colourful. The wooden floors are white, the couches are cream with coloured throw cushions, and even the desk is glass and stainless steel. The drapes and curtains are soft blue and lead out to the balcony, where there is a table for two to have coffee meetings if we need the air.

I bring Orchid to the desk and pull out the chair for her. I have things here I want to show her, and to be at the desk with the files at hand feels more natural. Like this isn't a big deal. I sit in the chair next to her, forgoing the opposite side of the desk. This isn't strictly a business meeting, and she might still be mad at me, or have questions for me.

I hand her the manila folder that's sitting on my desk waiting for her. 'This is for you. It's a sort of Thanksgiving and Christmas present all rolled into one. I've been working on it for a while, when things were quiet, so it's a good time to give it to you now. I know you like to have other things to ponder over when you're stressed.'

She opens the folder and I brace myself.

'Actually, you might want to read it at home. I know you're mad at me, and I don't want to give you something to soften the blow. I want you to have this, regardless. So just take this home and we can talk about it later.'

Orchid nods and closes the folder.

'Why did you bring me over to family breakfast? You could have given me this anytime.'

'I brought you to breakfast because I wanted to show you how families can be whatever you make them.'

'Meaning?'

'That I know you're scared of what hugely successful careers can do to families. Especially when there are jobs and contracts worth millions on the line. But not everyone puts their careers first.'

'One family breakfast for Thanksgiving doesn't prove anything, Max.'

137

'It's not just breakfast, Orchid. It's the idea behind it. Every day when we're in the same country at least, we eat as many meals together as we can. Breakfast and dinner always. Lunch is negotiable. Even when there is a busy job on—if you want to work early—you need to get up and work beforehand because you're expected at the breakfast table at eight a.m., regardless. Same for dinner.'

'So you have a happy family? Thanks for letting me know that it's just mine that sucks.'

Orchid looks genuinely upset.

'Hell no, it's not happy. Not always. You're looking at a family that has pulled through having a grandma for drunk and divorced parents, and a son who got shot up in war. But we pulled our shit together and made sure we tried. We tried to stick together, and we tried to keep a relationship going. And there were times at least one of us was depressed or not coping, but we didn't let that win. And we didn't use the guise of being too busy to draw a wedge between us. You could be happy with your family, Orchid. You might just have to be the one who pushes for what you want.'

'I don't even know what I want anymore,' she says.

'Sure you do, because you know exactly what you don't want for your future and your future kids. So start there. But you need to show up and be a part of the family for it to work.'

She nods. 'I could try. I guess I'm just scared they'll say no.'

'You got to try. And remember that no matter what happens, you still get to control how your life will be in the future, so don't freak out that you don't want to turn into them, and you won't.'

Orchid smiles and shuffles in her seat. 'Thanks for not freaking out when I started talking about our imaginary children. That one was a new cray-cray, even for me.' She clenches her teeth and smiles exaggeratedly.

'Well, since we can't go hiking, how about we go swimming?'

'It's October. I might have acclimatised to Irish weather, but LA's still not warm enough for me to swim in October.'

'Oh, Orchid. You really have been gone for too long.' I stand and pull her to her feet. 'This house has the outdoor pool, but my dad's house across the street has both indoor and outdoor. Plus, sauna and Jacuzzi. It's more of the, what did you call it? *Entertainment house*?'

    'As long as you don't make fun of my white bits. It's been far too long since I've sunbathed.'

    'Huh,' I say. 'Didn't know I was going to get to see your white bits.'

chapter twenty

Max

In the poolroom, I hit the heating up high and turn on the spotlights. The pool is warm, and Orchid and I gather up towels from the rack and position two loungers at the side of the pool. I have swim clothes down here and find some new swimmers in her size that will fit, and we change before sitting at the edge of the pool.

There's a mini bar here with snacks and drinks, and we get some nuts and water and set up one of the low tables between our loungers.

Orchid sinks her legs into the cool water, and I do the same. The wall to the left is a push back glass door that opens to the yard and the outside pool. But when it's closed, and you tint the windows, no one can see inside. So it's like our private room with one-way glass. We can still appreciate the outside views, but be closed off to ourselves.

'Why did your dad buy a house right next to his ex-wife? Isn't that a bit too close for comfort?'

I sit back on the lounger and cross my feet at my ankles. 'The thing about my parents is, I don't think they ever stopped loving each other.'

'That's kind of sad,' Orchid says. 'How long were they separated for?'

'Most of my life. I was three when they met and four when they married. Five when they divorced. So basically I've known them separate longer than together.'

'But you still call him Dad, even though they were together for such a short time?'

'He's always been my dad.' I swallow a lump in my throat. 'It wasn't until I became an adult that I really understood the responsibility he took on, even though I was not his.' I smile and it's a genuine smile. 'He never made me realise I was not his. I was old enough when they met to know that he wasn't my biological dad, but after the divorce, he always did everything a real father would have done. He had weekends and shared responsibility. He helped my mom with the day-to-day things, and even as a teenager, when I probably should have rebelled against the fact that he wasn't my dad, or even my stepdad anymore, he still showed up and acted like my dad. I guess I never thought to question it. I still don't. I think that's what real, unconditional love is.'

Orchid nods. 'The bond with a parent and child can be immense for some people, even if it's not a blood bond.'

I shake my head. 'No, I mean the love he still had for my mom. And by extension, that meant he loved me, too. He would do everything she needed, including loving her son—but whatever got in their way meant they just couldn't be together.'

'Why?' she asks. 'Surely love is enough?'

'I guess in real life, you need other things, too.'

'Did you ever ask them about it?'

'I asked my mom, and she said it was a combination of a lot of things in life that meant they couldn't be together for a while. That there were things about her that Dad didn't understand, but she knew that one day he would, and they would be together again.'

'Wait, she knew they would get back together? When was this?'

'I don't know, like five, six years ago maybe.'

Orchid raises her eyebrows and looks at the pool.

'What does that mean?' I ask her.

'Just.' She shrugs her shoulders. 'I mean, your dad had quite the reputation as a serial ... dater,' she says. 'That's got to be tough to watch.'

'Well, whatever happened, they worked it out in the end. Mom says she always knew Dad would be someone important in her life. That he was always there for her. Even when she didn't even realise she needed the help, he was there supporting her and falling in love with her. Even if you screw it up, like she did, and they divorced for twenty years, they were still in love with each other, they still were a part of each other's lives and my life, and Dad still loved us both enough, that despite not being my biological father, he stayed in my life. He did the weekend visits and parent-teacher conferences and moved into a house close by so he was always around for us. But despite all this, my mum stands by falling in love at first sight. And it's the reason I know you can't blame your family's career choices and the things that go with that as the reason that your relationship has suffered. You need to stop making excuses, Orchid, and face this grudge that you have against the people who are successful in LA.'

'Your parents love you, Orchid. And sometimes that's not enough. But if you want something more from them, you've got to learn how to ask for it. Maybe they think they're doing enough. They looked after you their whole life. They let you make your own decisions on whether you wanted to be a part of the family business. They let you go when you wanted to go your own way. They didn't hesitate to pull out all the stops to get your security team up to scratch on the other side of the world. Which, by the way, has cost almost the same as the entire setup here for them and your siblings combined. They didn't care about the bill, though, they just wanted you safe but happy in your own life. They didn't want anything uprooted for you. Maybe you're mad that their career impacts you, but they also do everything they can to help keep your life the way you want it.'

Orchid sinks her body into the pool and takes her time, rising up and pushing the water off her head and face. I follow her into the water, and we paddle around in silence for a few minutes. We've sat like this many times at home. When we're watching her baking shows or listening to music. Sometimes she just needs to sit and think. Sit in silence and contemplate everything that's going on in her head. I know her brain is working overload, that she's running through scenarios of what-ifs. She fidgets too much to be truly relaxed, and it didn't take me long to spot the signs of anxiety all over her life.

I can give her this. I can give her time and silence. And she seems to like it in my company. For the first few days in Dublin, she would shut herself in her office or pretend she needed a nap, just to get into the headspace. But now she knows she can get these moments to herself while I'm right there next to her.

As usual, she changes the subject completely.

'So what is this?' She points to the folder I gave her earlier, that's resting on the lounger next to her clothes.

'Don't you want to talk about Sabrina? She's been messing with your life, and she attacked you, Orchid.'

'I've spoken to my family. It's Ali I feel bad about. My friendship with Sabrina has been over for years. As soon as she started dating my brother and got herself a spot in the show, she stopped being my friend. I guess it's all she ever wanted, to be on TV, and she found her way in. Just a shame she had to break Ali's heart in the process.'

'And you. She must have broken something with you too, right? I mean, Orchid, she tried to have you killed. She paid Archie to attack you and terrorise you at home.'

Orchid nods. 'I know. But I'm dealing with it. And part of that healing is reconnecting with my old therapist and realising that there are a bunch of anxieties in my system right now. And while I'm here, I can take some of your advice too and work on rebuilding my relationship with my family.'

I swim to the edge of the pool, where Orchid's resting her arms, and perch on the side like she is.

'It was an idea for you. I know you wanted to start something like this, but you don't really have the time, so I thought I would put together a business plan for you, and you could see if it would be something that would actually work.'

'Max,' she gasps and leaps out of the pool. She dries her hands and wraps the towel around her. She scans the first sheet of paper and flips through the rest, looking at everything. 'This must have taken you forever.'

I shrug. 'Well, I hoped you would like it. Even if you don't use it, it would help you make the decision to let it go or not.'

Stalking inside Orchid's readers' group, as well as living in her house, has given me access to see so many of Orchid's desires and

143

dreams. She wants to take her career in so many directions and she doesn't have time for everything. I wanted to show her how she could chase some of her dreams, but hire people to help her. In the folder is the thing she talks most about with Ailish. Setting up a bookstore with merchandise and trinkets and book related gifts.

She knows it would need to be in Dublin, or in one of the larger towns to make it a workable business, but she always wanted to keep it close by that she could call in most days if needed. She also wants space for people to work and write, and maybe even run book clubs or writers' workshops from.

I've priced multiple locations and unit sizes for rent and rates, as well as asked the unit managers for foot traffic information and weekend trade. I've priced out the difference between hiring full-time vs. part-time staff to suit around a reduced store opening hours and also casual staffing for busier times like Christmas shopping and special events. Agency workers' rates are also included for her to look at, as that could be an option for starting out.

I looked up her Facebook groups and her stock records that Ailish let me have. I've worked out the items selling most, against the profit margin, and things that can be scalable to other generic book items that could be sold. There is information on prices for workshops and signing events, the box subscriptions that she loves, and the cost of rent and rates against the free events that she would make a priority like her charity nights and book club hosting. Orchid has loads of contacts with companies that she's made her personalised book swag with, and Ailish assisted me with costing these on a larger scale for store sales, and more generic pieces that could help reduce costs.

Orchid is still reading through everything and I'm waiting in the water when she tosses the folder closed and leaps towards me. She bends down at the pool edge and leans forward.

Her mouth lands on mine and the urgency to get her closer to me has my mouth crushing against hers. Her tongue over mine and her breath a part of me. Neither of us is breathing air that's not each other's and I slowly move backwards, taking Orchid into the pool with me. She straddles my legs and presses her body around mine, and I back her up and crush her against the hard wall edge of the pool.

I groan when she rubs herself over me and I let my hands dive deep into her hair. Falling over our faces, all I can smell is her.

'Orchid,' I breathe as the water laps around us and I know there are only scraps of fabric between us.

I pull her mouth back towards mine and in the slight break of contact, Orchid moves her hands between our bodies and rubs her hand over my dick. My eyes roll back and my dick hardens as I push my hips up towards her hand, wanting to feel her touch quicker than she's able to get my shorts down in the water.

I try to speak, but before I'm able to form a sentence, she has her hands down my shorts and her cool skin touching my dick is the softest and most calming thing I've ever felt.

'We should go somewhere, Orchid,' I say. 'Anyone could come in here. Cameron is still patrolling and—'

Orchid places her other hand over my mouth. 'Your room is across the street and far, far away,' she says.

I chuckle. 'Oh, Orchid, don't you think I at least have a bedroom over here too?'

Orchid looks me in the eye and pulls back slightly. She takes her hand out of my pants and says, 'Take me to bed, Max. Right now.'

I hold on to her ass and pull her tight against my dick. Grinding herself down on me, she smiles and I say, 'It's about bloody time, Orchid.'

In this house, my room is a standard bedroom, well as standard as it can get in Beverly Hills. It's next door to my dad's room, because mostly whenever I was here for the night, it was when I was a kid. The older I got, I stayed the night less, purely because most of my gaming stuff was at my mom's house. But my dad still kept this room for me. Even when I signed up to the army and my eventual injury retirement, the room has been decorated for the evolving me.

Although this one still holds touches of teenage Max on the walls. Darkened wallpaper and carpets, poster marks on the walls, and TV and sound system being the centre pride of the room. The bed is the only thing on my mind when I bring Orchid in here and close the door tightly behind us. I want her naked, and I want to see every part

145

of her. To kiss every part of her, here in the middle of the day, with the full brightness of the sun shining through the windows where I can see every part of her. I've already seen inside her soul, so it would be nice to see the rest of her.

'You know this is going to change everything, right?' I ask her with a smirk on my face, grabbing her hips and pulling her towards me.

'I kind of hope so,' she says.

I kiss her again and she pushes me back towards the bed. This time when I fall backwards, she stays standing and pulls her shirt over her head. When she untangles it from her wrist, she opens her bra clasp and tosses it to the ground. When she leans over me to lie down, I sit up and grab her nipple with my teeth.

She hisses and I move my hands over the waistband of her sweats. I dip my hands under her pants and grab hold of her panties, push them both down over her legs and have her naked.

Her breasts are warm in my mouth and I tease her nipple into a hard peak, to contrast the soft feel of her surround.

'I need you inside me.' She helps rip off my clothes and when our naked limbs tangle around each other, I know this is somewhere I never want to leave. The smell of Orchid over my body is intoxicating, but the feel of her wetness between her legs, rubbing on me, is something that's going to drive me wild forever.

I roll on top of her and when she arches her back to roll her hips up and wrap her legs around my ass, I slide inside her as slow as I can, drawing out the feel of her body tightening around mine and holding me there.

When I've sunk as far as I can go, I grab her legs and pull her tight against me, trying to go deeper, to claw inside as deep as I can get because I never want to leave, I never want to be away from her again.

'Fuck me, Max,' she whispers in my ear, and I do.

I hold one hand on the top of the headboard and the other onto her ass. I push fast and hard into her, riding her until her body is tight. Our movements have the headboard banging against the wall and the mattress squeaking, but it only makes me fuck her harder. She moans with the thrusts and I kiss her deep. I lean back onto my knees, still inside her, and grab her around her breasts. She moans out and places her hand on top of mine, squeezing it to hold her tighter. I bring her into a sitting position, back against the headboard, legs wrapped around me, and fuck her until she screams.

Lying in bed, staring at each other, I can't stop kissing her. Randomly, I'll pull her hand up to my mouth and kiss her fingers. And turn her palm over to kiss the inside of her hand. My dick's been hard since the moment I came and I'm ready to make love to her over and over again for what might be forever until I can get these feelings under control. I want to kiss her whole body and know the moment I move beyond her hands, it will end with my face between her legs and devouring her, so her taste will be ingrained in me forever.

'What would you say about staying in LA for a while?' she asks.

'What brought this on?'

'I was just thinking earlier about what you said. And now is a good opportunity to stay. My family has scaled back on their jobs and I have an excuse to stay home for a while. I have my laptop with me, and that's all I basically need for work.'

'Sounds like a good idea.'

She turns on her side. 'You said that Cameron was going to be in charge of my security—does that mean when I go back home, you won't be coming?'

'Officially as your security, no. I won't.'

She swallows.

'But I was thinking about finding somewhere close by to rent for a while.'

'In Dublin?' she asks.

I nod. 'Near you, yes. I want this too, Orchid. I just want to do it right. I can't be on the job with someone I'm in love with. It wouldn't keep you as safe as you might think. But I can run a lot of my company remotely and fly back here when I need to. So if you wanted to turn this into a relationship'—I look her in the eyes—'then let's do it. Let's go back to what we had, working near each other during the day and spending the evenings and weekends together.'

147

She shrugs. 'I mean, we were practically an old couple as it was.'

I laugh and pull her in for a hug, but she pushes against me.

'Do you mean it or was it a general statement?'

'Mean what?' I ask.

She looks down at the bed. 'You said someone you're in love with.'

Jesus, I did. And she didn't freak out.

I put my hand under her hair, around the back of her head, and pull her head up to look at me.

'I sure did.' I smile softly at her. 'I kind of fell in love with you the first time I saw you.'

She smiles. 'That's impossible, Max.'

'No, it's not. It's the most genuine feeling I've ever had.'

Orchid runs her hand over my face, looking into my eyes. 'You could be a romance author,' she teases.

There is a harsh bang on my bedroom door and Orchid jumps. We're naked, on a bed, postcoital, and no sheets or covers nearby in case someone comes in here.

'Hold on,' I call out.

Orchid's face reddens. 'OMG, who the hell heard us?' she hisses.

Shit.

I never thought of that.

The only way someone would know we were in here would be if they heard us.

'Have a development. The Rock family have asked for you both to be at their house,' Cameron calls out. There's a pause before he speaks again. 'I've left your clothes out here. I'll wait out front.'

I give Cameron a second to make himself scarce and open the door to retrieve our clothes. Cameron really needs a raise. He's bundled up the clothes we left at the pool and also brought up some towels.

I toss Orchid her clothes and she tries to hold in her laughter as she hops on one leg, trying to get back into her sweatpants.

chapter twenty-one

Max

Once we're dressed and Orchid runs her fingers through her hair to smooth out the just-fucked look, I pull her in for a kiss and run my tongue over hers. I want to taste her all day, and if we had to get dressed and out of bed, I want to be touching her as much as I can.

It only takes ten minutes to make it out of my dad's driveway and over to Orchid's family home. We grew up so close to each other, but a million miles away, too. In high school, Orchid never noticed me. There were a lot of kids from Hollywood parents, so there was never a scandal or chatter about who's kid was in school. I don't think she even realised we were at the same school at the same time, let alone that I was friends with one of her brothers. When you're a teenager, three years of an age difference is a lifetime.

And by that time, the Rock TV show was already on air, and Orchid had started to distance herself from her family.

Waiting for us, in the Rock formal dining room at a table big enough to seat the whole family and security team, are Orchid's parents. They are flanked by her two sisters, Adhara and Coco, and their husbands, whom I'm never met before. Her brother Ali is there as well as Elvis, who used to help coach the younger kids' track in high school—aka me. Elvis stands up and gives me a tight hug and a slap on the arm.

The six nieces and nephews can be seen playing in the backyard with a nanny and one of my security guys on the edge of the garden.

James, my business partner, is suited and booted at the other end of the table and Cameron takes the seat next to him.

When Orchid sits, I take the seat next to her, bracing for the development.

'What's happened?' I ask.

'Sabrina is being held on psych charges and even if her lawyer gets her out of those, we have enough evidence that's been handed to the police to hold her on stalking, threatening behaviour, arson, and assault.'

Ali chews on his lips and there is a solemn feeling around the table.

'What am I supposed to tell the kids?' he asks.

Orchid moves her chair, but Coco makes it over to Ali before her and takes his hand. 'We'll figure it out,' she says.

James continues speaking. 'It's getting worse. If you don't want to hear it, I can speak to the others without you.'

'I want to know everything you do,' Ali says. 'We all do.' He looks at his parents and his siblings and everyone nods and there is a collection of agreeing murmurs.

'There were further developments with the man, Archie, in Dublin. Following his interviews and investigations, I would suggest, evident enough, that the threat against the family is now at its lowest level.'

There is a collection of sighs and relief around the table at the news, except for Orchid.

James shakes his head. 'I've been on the phone with the investigating psychologist since six this morning and it needs to be confirmed, but it looks like Sabrina orchestrated an attack on Orchid using Archie in Dublin.'

James looks at his sheet. 'Best we can decipher is that Sabrina developed an obsession over Orchid during early teenage years and started targeting her family to get closer to her when her friendship wasn't enough.

'And when Orchid distanced herself from her family, it made Sabrina's obsession volatile. When her threats weren't having an impact, and she couldn't get physically near to her in Ireland, she started an obsession with tormenting the family and found someone to help her in Ireland—that's where Archie came in.

'Her mental state is unstable. She feels that it was her right to find you and return you to the family home. Apparently, a lot of her rage comes from you changing your name and hiding from who you really are to the Rock family business.'

'Jesus Christ, Orchid,' Elvis says. 'You really know how to get people obsessing over you.'

Bernard clips his son over the side of the ear. 'This is serious.'

'I know,' he says. 'Just trying to ease some tension.'

Orchid leans back in her chair, deflated and exhausted with the news. She holds so much inside, it's sometimes necessary to see her crash.

'I was thinking about staying a while,' she tells her family, looking at her mom first, then her dad.

Her mom reaches for her. 'That would be nice. It's been so long since we've had you in the country for more than a few days. And Ali will need our help, too.' Astrid takes her son's hand in her free one. 'We'll pull through this as a family.'

Orchid nods. 'I think it's time I actually made room in my work schedule to do the family thing.' Orchid's voice is almost a whisper, and I get up from the chair to leave them together. James gathers his notes and he leaves, too.

I can hear the chatter behind me as one of Orchid's sisters tells her how she needs to schedule off a specific day a month for a family sleepover at home, where they all come for dinner and spend the evening watching movies and crashing together. I smile and know that there is so much more for Orchid to come. She loves her schedules, and I can just imagine her making appointments to spend time with each one of her family—eventually, it will just turn into her everyday routine.

I'm only at the front door when Orchid chases after me.

'I just wanted to check where you'll be?' she asks.

'I'm heading back to my mom's, but call me when you're done here. I want to hang out, if you have the energy later. It's bound to be an exhausting few hours sorting through this lot with your brother.'

151

She nods. 'Okay. I just mean long term. Or in the next few weeks or months or whatever. What country will you be in?'

I realise what she's asking and I smile. 'I'll be where you are.'

'Good. 'Cause I want to be where you are too.'

'And one day, you're going to want to move back to Dublin and pick up your writing routine and live on your land with no dramas.'

Orchid nods. 'I will. But I'd really love it if we can share that office space again.'

I take a step forward, run my hands around the back of her head, and softly twist her hair in my hand. When I pull her body flush against mine, I whisper into her ear again, 'I'll be where you are. Forever.' And then I kiss her. Forever.

a note from the author

THANK YOU FOR READING

Don't forget to leave a review on your platform of choice. It really does help out readers and Indie authors alike.

If you're not already following me on social media:
www.facebook.com/bronamillsauthor
www.instagram.com/bronamillsauthor
or join up my readers group on facebook: Brona Mills Finding Time for Everything

If you want to keep up to date on news, blogs and releases, head on over to my website
www.bronamills.com and sign up to my newsletter.

War and books

Other books by the author

Time for an adventure Series:

A Time For Everything   The Same Time

Coming 2022:
Mirror Mirror   Once Upon a time Loop

Saving Dystopia series:

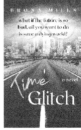

Printed in Great Britain
by Amazon